THE
QUADRA
CONNECTION

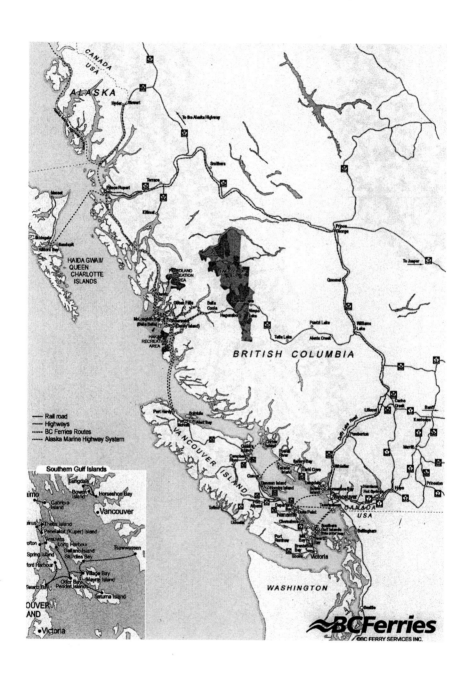

THE
QUADRA
CONNECTION

A West Coast Novel of
Adventure and Intrigue

Robert Whitfield

Strategic Book Publishing and Rights Co.

Strategic Book Publishing and Rights Co.
12620 FM 1960, Suite A4-507
Houston, TX 77065
www.sbpra.com

ISBN: 978-1-61204-780-5
Book Design by Julius Kiskis

20 19 18 17 16 15 14 13 12   1 2 3 4 5

Dedication

This book is dedicated to James C. Robertson, Robert C. Hele,
and all the fine Marine Engineers I sailed with during
my days at sea; and in particular, to all of the dedicated
Members of the Royal Canadian Mounted Police
who serve so faithfully in
British Columbia and throughout Canada.

Contents

Part II – The Distributors

Part III– The Bottom Line

Acknowledgments

Sincere appreciation to Patricia Caldwell, Bob and Diane Hele, Jeannie Thomson, Alice Sontag and Patricia Salmon for their review and comments on the early drafts.

Many thanks to the entire support team at Strategic Book Publishing and, in particular, to Edit Manager Beverly Porter and Editor Julius Kiskis for their invaluable assistance in producing this work

Part I

✹

The Imporrters

One

The wind-driven October rain blew in successive gusty sheets up the street from the harbor, so heavy at times that the streetlights produced only a dim glow on the sidewalks. The blinking red neon sign, not very bright because of the driving rain, continued to identify the Harbor House Hotel two blocks up from the waterfront. Things were much brighter inside. The Saturday night crowd was just about at full volume at 11:00 p.m., with the raucous conversations competing with the folk music from the band. The waiters hustled back and forth from the bar to the tables with brimming pitchers of beer slopping onto their trays and the house was full to overflowing as the young crowd of loggers, fishermen and mill workers partied in the middle of their much deserved weekend break.

Jack Martin, full time barkeeper and part time philosopher, noted with satisfaction the almost steady stream of movement between the tables and the restrooms, indicating that business was at its Saturday night best. He also noted the unobtrusive entry of an RCMP constable dressed in foul weather gear standing just inside the doorway, surveying the crowd and looking for signs of impending trouble and obviously underage drinkers. Satisfied with what she saw, she gave Jack the thumbs-up sign and headed back out into the stormy night, hoping that none of the cheerful bunch of singers and storytellers ended up wrapped around a tree in their pickup trucks on their way home at 3:00 a.m. It would be a real treat to get through a wintry Saturday night in Port Alberni without having to file accident reports detailing serious injuries or fatalities.

At one corner table as far from the foot stomping band as possible, Jack noted five men who seemed to be talking seriously. Three were obviously fishermen, based on their clothes and their deeply tanned and weathered faces. The other two acted like businessmen who had deliberately dressed down to look as though they really belonged in a noisy, crowded West Coast pub on a Saturday night. As the conversation continued, one of the businessmen quickly passed a large brown manila envelope to the most grizzled looking fisherman of the three in exchange for a smaller more weathered looking one. Jack finally figured out what was going on, the boat owners were selling a commercial fishing license. Another one of the big packing companies was taking advantage of the bargains made available because independent boats could no longer make a decent living catching the few commercial quality fish still available during the short season.

Sure enough, after a barely decent interval of meaningless conversation, the two got up, shook hands all around, and headed for the door putting on their totally inadequate, fashionable raincoats as they went. The three remaining at the table, visibly relaxed and smiling, shouted for another pitcher and got down to some serious drinking. After an hour or so the three got up, put on their slickers and headed somewhat unsteadily to the door hollering a cheerful goodnight to Jack as they left. Walking downhill towards the waterfront, heading directly into the wind and rain, they skipped the almost obligatory detour into the alley for a piss against the brick wall, and continued weaving on.

Strangely enough, as they got closer to fisherman's wharf where the boats were heaving up and down in the wind-generated swells, they picked up their pace and walked purposefully down the float to the *Glory Bee*. Captain Oley went straight to the wheelhouse and started the engine while his sons let go the lines fore and aft, then hopped on board. With radar turning but no navigation lights or whistle signals, the boat backed out into the harbor just after 2:00 a.m., turned, and headed down the inlet towards the open seas of the Pacific. Eventually, about a mile down the channel, the navigation lights came on, but no departure report was called into the Vessel Traffic System (VTS) controller at Tofino.

Two

The deep beat of the slow-speed Sulzer diesel and the whining of the turbocharger gradually grew louder as the increasing engine speed began to accelerate the refrigerated container ship *Gran Ecuadoro* after it had stopped to pick up a pilot near Bamfield. As the pilot came onto the bridge, he was somewhat out of breath after climbing up the ladder from the pilot boat to the main deck and then up six more flights of stairs. He introduced himself to the captain, checked the ship's position on the chart and the electronic displays, and then reported the ship to VTS as inbound in the Alberni Inlet proceeding to a dock in Port Alberni. VTS gave him the clearance to proceed and reported no other traffic in the inlet. The pilot reviewed the weather forecast with the bridge watch; dark, rainy and windy as usual; and then went over the voyage plan on his laptop with the captain and the second officer. He then gave a new course to steer and settled into his favorite corner at a bridge front window staring ahead into the gloom.

Far below in the machinery control room which was somewhat insulated from the heat and noise of the engine room upper level where it was located, third engineer, Manuel Ortega, leaned back in his upholstered swivel chair. The chair had recently been liberated from a broken container shipment of furniture and was the newest item of equipment in the machinery spaces. With his feet up on the control console he occasionally gave a cursory glance at the main engine gauges, and then continued to read the worn copy of *Hustler* Magazine that he had reluctantly put down when the ship began the maneuvers to pick up the pilot. Behind him at the desk Hector Vargas, the oiler on watch, was making a fresh pot of coffee before heading out to take the engine room logbook readings. Twenty years ago when the ship was new and everything worked the way the Lloyds surveyors expected it to, the automated engine room was unattended and mundane tasks such as taking log readings happened automatically. Now, with most of the automation system worn beyond repair, the owners reluctantly provided watch keepers and paid for just enough maintenance to keep the plant operating while they squeezed as much profit as possible out of the ship before being forced by high insurance rates to sell it for scrap.

Hector finished his domestic chores and, with a casual wave of his clipboard to the third engineer, stepped out into the heat and noise of the engine room to begin his data collection. While circling around the main engine top level, which was in sight of the control room, he meticulously recorded the jacket water outlet temperatures, the turbocharger oil levels, and the miscellaneous thermometer and pressure gauge readings for the auxiliaries. As he moved down to the lower levels where he was out of sight, his speed increased and his data recording became more casual. Finally, when he reached the lowest level and went through the shaft alley door, he was almost running, although he did check the shaft bearing temperatures on his way down the long tunnel.

After checking the stern tube temperature, Hector climbed up the vertical escape ladder to the lobby outside the steering gear room and the stewards' storerooms, carefully closing and dogging the watertight hatch behind him. He then went into the noisy room containing the steering engine, closing that door behind him as he went. Completing a quick check of the steering equipment and recording temperatures, pressures and fluid levels, he then did a strange thing. With a great deal of effort, he lifted up two sections of deck plating and climbed down to the tank top level. While stooped over, he shined his flashlight around quickly locating four large army duffel bags that were so completely filled that they formed round, tightly packed cylinders. The green canvas bags were wrapped in heavy waterproof black plastic, sealed over a layer of foam flotation material that was applied to permit the bags to float upright. The canvass strap handle on the top of each bag was wrapped with a reflective white tape. With much grunting, groaning and profuse swearing, he managed to wrestle each of the four sixty kilogram bags up to the deck plate level in the compartment and then replaced the floor plates.

Hector took a couple of minutes to catch his breath and then switched off the normal lighting in the room. With only the dim emergency lights to guide him, he climbed up another vertical escape ladder, quietly opened the hatch, and climbed out onto the chilly, wet, deck outside. He carefully looked around to make sure that no one was out there having a smoke. Then he went back down the ladder and proceeded to lift each duffel bag by the handle and drag it over beside the ladder. With almost superhuman effort, he progressively lifted all four bags to the main deck and dragged them over to the aft railing above the propeller. Once again looking around for anyone who might be watching, he gave each bag a sharp smack below the handle to activate the low-power VHF beacon transmitter inside, then lifted the bag over the stern rail to drop it into the ship's wake far below.

Much relieved that his physical ordeal was over for this trip, Hector reentered the ship's interior through the door on the aft deck that led into the galley which was deserted at this early hour. He then proceeded to pick the lock on the bakery door and filled a tray purloined from the galley-serving counter with a selection of rolls and pastries prepared the evening before. This task completed, he rushed along the passageway to the machinery casing entrance, opened the door, and quickly descended the stairs to the machinery control room. Thinking about the significant bonus which awaited him at the end of the voyage, he entered the control room to have the Third greet him with, "Where the fuck have you been? Oh, okay, okay, let's see what you got on the tray for me." Hector just smiled again contemplating the large amount of cash he would receive as soon as the ship arrived in Chile.

On the bridge, the second officer scanning the radar display called out, "Contact bearing 10 degrees to port, range 5 miles." The pilot acknowledged the report and scanned ahead with his binoculars. Seeing nothing, he came over to the radar display, looked at the small size of the target, and concluded that it was a fishing vessel that had not bothered to check in with VTS. After a few minutes, he visually identified the boat by its navigation lights and realized that if both vessels maintained their course a harmless port-to-port passing would occur. He attempted to raise the boat on the VHF to confirm this, but got no response. Shortly thereafter, he noted in the log that the fishing vessel *Glory Bee* had passed to port at 3:10 a.m. at a distance of one-quarter mile.

Immediately after passing *Gran Ecuadoro*, the *Glory Bee*

rapidly turned to port and then proceeded down the inlet directly in the wake of the much larger vessel. With the VHF tuned to a little used channel to detect chirping beacon signals, and the two crew members up on the foredeck scanning the sea ahead with powerful five-cell flashlights, they eventually managed to locate the four large objects bobbing up and down in the sea with their reflective handles barely breaking the surface. After considerable maneuvering, grunting, swearing, snagging with boat hooks and sheer hard work, the two managed to land the four heavy duffel bags on board. Dragging them down the deck, they lifted them into the fish hold and, using a rake, covered them with layers of ice while the boat increased to top speed and continued past the Bamfield Light to the open sea ahead.

Considering the course they had been on, instead of turning south towards the Straits of Juan de Fuca and a sheltered passage to Victoria or Vancouver, *Glory Bee* surprisingly turned to the northwest and soon encountered the giant swells of the open Pacific. Rolling abysmally in the open waters off the west coast of Vancouver Island, the small vessel took the sheltered inside passages whenever possible but could not avoid long stretches of unsheltered ocean when passing Estevan Point and Cape Cook. After many gut wrenching hours Captain Oley finally concluded that he could not get around Cape Scott at the north end of the island until the weather abated, so he reluctantly turned into Quatsino Sound and anchored near Winter Harbor. There, he and the boys got several hours of much needed sleep before continuing their unusual circumnavigation of Vancouver Island.

Three

The reflection of the moon on the light chop breaking the surface of the sea indicated the direction that the cold breeze was blowing from as the waves splashed onto the Quathiaski Cove shoreline. From a car with the front window rolled down in the terminal parking lot, the sound of the diesel engines on the approaching ferry could be heard, even though the ship was still out of sight behind the point. The departure lanes in the lot had several cars lined up waiting to board the 1000 p.m. trip across Discovery Passage to Campbell River. While too late on a Friday night for just a quick visit to Vancouver Island, obviously some folks were leaving Quadra Island for a longer weekend get away. On the other side of the lot, facing the exit lanes from the ferry ramp was a patrol car with the vehicle markings of the Royal Canadian Mounted Police. Inside the car sat Constable Level 2, Johnny Novak who was thoroughly enjoying his recent posting to the detachment after completing an incredibly busy and hectic field coaching program in Burnaby Detachment. Johnny, just one year and a few months away from the small town of Humboldt, Saskatchewan, had not liked the fast pace of the big city environment in the Vancouver Region since he had usually been too tired on his days off to enjoy any big city pleasures. The small Quadra Island community was just

11

the right size as far as he was concerned.

Johnny was parked at the terminal to practice his skills of observation, checking for anything that seemed unusual among the people or vehicles coming off the ferry on this late October Friday evening. While nominally there to provide assistance if required, things were still quiet on the nightwatch and it was an ideal time to advertise to any arriving visitors that there was a police presence on the island. Since tourist season was over, most visitors now came on business of one sort or another and the detachment personnel liked to stay up to date on just who was around and why. Johnny was feeling just a little more important than usual tonight, since the more Senior Constable Ed Brewer and his wife were taking a long weekend off in Nanaimo. This left him as second in command, the only constable available to assist the NCOIC.

As the lights of the approaching ferry became visible, Johnny resumed his previous thoughts about the very attractive waitress at the coffee shop near the terminal. He had developed the habit of dropping in for coffee regularly and she seemed quite friendly whenever he came in. The problem was that he was not supposed to socialize with the residents in the detachment area and had not figured out a way to approach her with his idea of a trip to Campbell River for a dinner-date on his day off.

His daydream ended abruptly with the sound of the ferry engines going astern as the ship eased into the ramp. The lines were secured and the ramp dropped to allow the cars to slowly come ashore just as he assumed his posture of casual disinterest in the unloading process. The next to last car off got his attention. A gray Ford Explorer with two very well-dressed men inside eased by him on the way to West Road. The business suits and ties did not fit the pattern for normal island attire on a late Friday night. Unless they were about to make an immediate business visit on arrival, almost everyone would take their ties off when they first got on the ferry. And there was certainly no place open at this hour that would be even remotely interested in a formal sales call or business meeting. Johnny opened his notebook and quickly jotted down the time, date, automobile make, model, color and license number, and then returned the book to his shirt pocket. He also decided to have a careful look around during his night patrol of the island to see if he could at least find out where they were staying.

After another brief stop for coffee and a shy "hello" to the waitress, his third since starting his shift at 6:00 p.m., he began his leisurely patrol over all the island roads, He stopped in the built up areas to check the front doors of business establishments and cruised through the parking lots of the bigger places to check behind the buildings. Tonight he went out of his way to check every resort, motel, and bed and breakfast parking spot from Lighthouse Road to Heriot Bay, on both the front and back roads, trying to locate the gray Explorer with no success. Since no radio calls had come in from the Courtenay Communications 911 Center to give him something more exciting to do, he became somewhat obsessed with the idea of finding the visiting car. After calling Courtenay to advise them that he was continuing routine patrol, he started out again. This time he paid more attention to residential driveways, and most of the back roads in the close-in areas. Still no luck. He knew the car had to be on the island somewhere, since the last ferry to Cortes Island had sailed before the vehicle had arrived on Quadra, and it was highly unlikely that they had gone right back to Campbell River on the last ferry trip of the night.

Serious now, he headed out towards the north end of the island out Bold Point Road, checking all of the side roads and trails that he could navigate. Cruising slowly down the road leading to the beaches at the north end of Heriot Bay, looking down any access lane leading straight onto a sandy beach, he caught a moonlit glimpse of front bumper chrome as he coasted by. Excited by his discovery and forgetting all of his recent training procedures, he continued on and turned into a driveway leading up the hill to a long abandoned cabin. He made sure his vehicle could not be seen from the road and then walked quickly and quietly back to the beach lane carrying his portable searchlight. Sure enough, as he stood on the road looking down the lane he could just make out the front end of the Explorer which had backed down to the beach as far as possible without the risk of getting stuck in the soft sand.

Walking silently down the lane to the halfway point to the beach he stopped, amazed. The moon shining periodically through the passing clouds illuminated a strange scene. The bow of a skiff was pulled up on the beach with a man dressed in black coveralls standing in front holding a large duffel bag up on end. A similar bag was lying on the sand at the back of the vehicle, while two other men dressed in black struggled to lift a loaded, very heavy duffel bag into the back of the vehicle. Just offshore, drifting slowly was a fishing vessel without lights. The wheelhouse door was open and someone was watching the scene unfolding on the beach. Striding boldly past the front of the Explorer, Johnny shone the light into the eyes of the men at the back of the vehicle and shouted, "Freeze, hands where I can see them, explain what you're doing!" Overcome with surprise, everyone on the beach did stop what they were doing and stared right at him. Johnny didn't hear the soft footsteps in the sand behind him, didn't hear the silenced cough of the 45-magnum projectile leaving the barrel, and was dead before he and the flashlight hit the ground.

"Holy shit, what did you do that for?" one of the men at the car yelled at the shooter who was pushing his weapon into the front of his coveralls.

"Shut the fuck up," was the reply. "You in the boat, throw that bag out onto the beach and go get a shovel from your yacht out there."

"Hey," said the other man at the back of the car while turning toward the skiff, "I'll go with him!"

"No you won't, dumb ass, finish loading and then start raking the sand clear of footprints."

The gunman then grabbed Johnny by the ankles and dragged his body to a soft sandy area above the high tide line just below the trees. The skiff returned and the shovel was passed to the gunman who immediately began digging a shallow grave in the sand. As his partner was shoving the last duffel bag into position in the back of the vehicle, the other two were back in the skiff furiously paddling towards the fishing boat, which had moved to meet them. The moment the two were aboard and the skiff secured, the *Glory Bee* took off at full throttle towards Cape Mudge.

The two men remaining on the beach dragged Johnny on his back into the hollowed out area in the sand. One proceeded to cover him up while the other, beginning at the shoreline where the skiff had been, began to meticulously rake the sand to match the untouched portions of the beach area. After raking the grave area and covering their footprints as they moved towards the SUV, each opened a front door and removed a black plastic garbage bag from inside. They then removed their rubber boots and coveralls, stuffing them into the bags. One got into the vehicle and moved it half way up the lane while the other, barefoot with pant legs rolled up, raked the final footprints and tire tracks away. With the full garbage bags tied shut and placed on the second seat, the men finished transforming themselves into business executives once more, moved the SUV onto the road, and proceeded down to the driveway where Johnny had concealed his car. They backed in and parked, but not so far up the drive that they saw the patrol vehicle. There they sat, dozing and listening to the radio, waiting until an hour before the first morning ferry trip to Campbell River. During their leisurely drive back to the terminal, they made a detour behind the school and deposited a rake, a shovel and two full plastic garbage bags, one with gun and shoulder holster, into the covered dumpster.

Four

The alarm buzzed loudly at 5:30 a.m. Corporal Ken Mullet RCMP, NCOIC of the Quadra Island detachment, rolled over quickly and shut it off before it woke up his wife. He then paddled naked into the bathroom to begin his regular morning routine of toilet, teeth, shave and shower. Emerging clean and refreshed he quickly put on his uniform, picked up his boots, and walked out of the room in his stocking feet, quietly closing the bedroom door behind him. He went downstairs to the living room and sat down to put on his boots, relishing the thought of that first cup of freshly made coffee waiting for him in the detachment office. He then crossed the entry hall by the front door of the detachment quarters and opened the office door hollering, "Top of the morning, Johnny" as he walked in. He stopped in his tracks in bewilderment. The office was dark and empty, and there was no smell of freshly brewed coffee in the air. He quickly flipped on the light switch and went back to the two tiny cells in the room next to his office and looked in there. He saw nothing at all. He then went to the office logbook at the front desk, no entries since 8:00 p.m. the previous evening. He checked the answering machine for messages. He heard nothing. Finally, he looked out the window to the parking lot at the side of the building. There was Quadra 1, and the four by four, but the spot for Quadra 2 was empty. *If he's asleep out there someplace I'll have his ass,* he thought to himself, *but he's never done this before, or even seemed particularly sleepy in the morning. I'd better find out where the hell he is before things start to get busy around here.*

Ken went to the desk and picked up the radio mike. "Quadra 1, Quadra 2: what's your 10-20?"

There was silence, no response to this location request.

"Quadra 1, Courtenay: what was Quadra 2's last 10-20?" he asked the Courtenay communications dispatcher.

"Courtenay, Quadra 1: Quadra 2 reported 10-8 on patrol from the ferry terminal at 10:15 p.m. last night, no calls since then."

"Quadra 1, 10-4 Courtenay, thanks. Please try to raise Quadra 2; I can't seem to get him from here."

Ken then switched frequencies.

"Quadra 1, all Campbell River units, did anyone hear from Quadra 2 during the night?" Fourteen responses, including highway patrol units, produced no clue. Now Ken was getting seriously concerned and even the thought of fresh coffee was almost forgotten. He rushed up to the bedroom and gently shook Marge awake.

"I've got to go out for awhile, honey, I can't locate Johnny. Could you please cover the radio and the phones in the office until the clerk comes in or until I get back? I'm going to look around to see what or whom he got himself into. If he comes in, or calls, tell him he's in big trouble and let me know right away."

"Did I just hear you tell me you've lost a constable overnight?" Marge asked sleepily. "What kind of a Boy Scout leader are you anyway?"

She gave him a big, good morning kiss and he went quickly downstairs and out to the car.

"Quadra 1, Courtenay: I'm 10-8 from the detachment."

"Courtenay, Quadra 1: 10-4. No response from Quadra 2, I'll log him 10-7 out of service. Let me know if there's a change."

Ken started out at the ferry terminal at 6:30 a.m., just after the first sailing of the day had left, and unknowingly repeated Johnny's search pattern of last night with no results. It was a cold but clear morning and the sun would be up soon, so he made the trip to the north end of the island quickly, then turned around and began a slow systematic search of every driveway, trail and side road that he came to. He tried calling Quadra 2 on the radio periodically, but then stopped doing that when he realized that Courtenay dispatch would be wondering what the hell was going on.

By 8:30 a.m., he was heading down the road past the beach access lane and the driveway where Johnny had left his car. He reached the end of the road and turned around. Still nothing. *One more cruise around this island and I'll have to request help,* he thought. *This is crazy, he can't just disappear into thin air and take the car with him.* He started slowly back up the road and passing the driveway to the old cabin he suddenly stopped, backed up, and decided to go up to the end of this drive and every other one he came to until he found Quadra 2.

Thirty seconds after this big decision, he saw the car. In the shade of the trees, the morning frost hadn't yet melted off the windows, so it was obvious that the unit had been sitting there for some time. Ken quickly got out of his car and went up to the Quadra 2 driver's side window, fully expecting to find Johnny asleep inside. No one. He walked the rest of the way up the driveway to the abandoned cabin and looked all around the area, calling Johnny's name. No reply. He then went back to Quadra 2, opened the door, removed the ignition key, and locked the car.

Looking for footprints now, Ken slowly walked down the driveway to the road, then up towards the beach lane. At the entrance to the lane, Ken saw fresh tire tracks indicating that a car had recently turned onto the road from the beach. He also saw faint boot prints in the sand at the side of the lane heading towards the beach, but nothing coming back towards the road. Walking slowly, careful not to disturb anything he saw on the ground and with the cover of his holster unsnapped to make his weapon readily available, he cautiously moved to the beach. No one. The sun was up, the water was beautiful and reflected the sunshine in the crisp morning air, seagulls flew in circles looking for breakfast, the waves lapped the smooth sandy beach, but there was no goddamned sign of Constable Johnny Novak. "Shit," Ken exclaimed to no one in particular.

Looking up and down the beach, Ken finally noticed that the contours of the sand were peculiar. From the end of the lane to the water's edge, and to five meters or so on either side, the sand looked too smooth. In fact, it looked freshly raked in the same way that the tourist beaches are groomed in Vancouver. Looking back up the beach to his left near the tree line, Ken noticed a two-meter long depression in the sand, nicely raked, as was the sand leading back to where he stood. Suddenly realizing what he was looking at, he raced to the end of the depression and began digging furiously in the sand with both hands, like a dog anxious to hide a bone in the dirt. Continuing to scoop out the hole, he touched something hard and smooth and identified the black toe of a boot. Then two boots, RCMP issue, with feet still inside them. Ken drew back, turned aside and retched, but there was nothing to bring up. He got up, staggered over to lean against a tree and tried to grasp what he was dealing with. *A young constable murdered in a quiet detachment, on a quiet night, no motive, no suspects, no damned reason at all,* he thought, *and me without the slightest idea of what could have happened. How can I explain this to his family, or to anyone else?*

The seagulls began to wheel around the hole in the sand and one landed to begin to check it out. Ken rushed over and filled it up, made the sign of the cross, and with tears running down his cheeks rushed back to his car and picked up the radio microphone. Then he paused, and began to think more clearly. *No one living on this island would have done something like this, I know all the people here. Tourist season is long since over. Someone has recently arrived, was up to no good, and Johnny caught him. But who, and doing what? One thing is for sure, if the press gets hold of this and word gets out, we'll never catch the low-life son of a bitch who whacked him.*

Five

Ken started his car and backed down to the road, then moved up to park in front of the beach lane. He got out with a roll of yellow police crime scene tape and closed off the entrance to the lane by stretching tape between two trees and tying it off. He then walked back and tied off the entrance to the driveway leading up to Quadra 2. Knowing that he had to report this by landline telephone and not by radio, he lost no time in heading back towards the office. As he rushed towards West Road, he suddenly slammed on the brakes and pulled into a driveway. He hurried up the front steps of the bungalow in the neatly tended garden, and rang the bell. He rang again twice and then once again. After a considerable pause a woman in a loosely tied bathrobe opened the door cautiously, saw who it was, and quickly ushered him in.

"Ken, its only 9:30 a.m.," she said. "Steve is working the afternoon shift and we didn't get to bed until after 2:00 a.m., what in the world do you want?"

"I'm really sorry, Paula," Ken replied. "I have to talk to Steve for just a minute and then I'll be on my way."

Steve and Paula Mercer had lived on Quadra Island all of their lives, and had made a pretty good living with commercial fishing until the salmon stocks dried up and he had to surrender his license and sell the boat. Fortunately, Steve had worked in the towboat industry in his younger days and his 500 Ton Master's Certificate qualified him for a job as a deck officer with the BC Ferry System. Steve was currently working as a mate on the Campbell River - Quadra Island route and would have seen every vehicle coming over to the island last night. Paula turned the coffee maker on, which made Ken realize just how thirsty he was, and then she banged on the bathroom door.

"Steve, Ken is here to talk to you. He said if I don't get my turn in there soon he's going to break in and take you away."

Steve came out laughing, his hair still wet. He gave Paula a light slap on the bottom and pushed her towards the bathroom.

"All right woman, you win. With reinforcements like Ken to help you, I don't stand a chance."

He waited a minute and then poured two cups of coffee. He put them on the table and then turned to look intently at Ken.

"You look a little flustered this morning, sheriff, you loose your horse or what?"

"I'm investigating something that went down last night Steve," Ken replied, "but I can't tell you much about it yet. I could really use some input on anyone different that you might have seen, or anything that seemed unusual during your trips yesterday."

Steve sipped on his coffee and thought about it. Since the mate is in charge of loading and unloading the ferry passengers and vehicles, he was in a position to observe almost everyone that came on board and subsequently left the small vessel.

"Well, it was pretty quiet last night," he said thoughtfully. "Traffic was light in both directions even for October. There were the usual number of folks going over to Campbell River and points south for the weekend, and the residents coming back home after a day in the big town. I did notice one thing that was a little unusual for this time of year, though. On the 9:30 p.m. trip out of Campbell River there was a gray Ford Explorer on board, with two men that looked like CEOs of a major corporation judging by the way they were dressed. Expensive suits, fancy ties, the works. Didn't get out of the SUV or pay any attention to anything around them. I can't imagine whom they were going to see on a Friday night at this time of year. I've never seen them traveling around here before either."

"Whoa, just a minute Ken," Steve suddenly exclaimed. "Your new guy must have seen them, he was parked at the terminal watching the cars that come off that trip. He seemed to be paying close attention when they went past him. Why don't you check with him?"

"Thanks, Steve. That's really a big help. Johnny wasn't around when I started out this morning, but I can check the logbook. Thanks for the coffee and the hospitality."

He quickly finished off his coffee, got up, shook Steve's hand and headed for the front door. On the way, he stopped and tapped on the bathroom door saying, "Thanks Paula, I'm out of here. See you folks again soon." Then he rushed to the car and headed off down the road to the ferry terminal, passing the detachment office on the way.

"What do you suppose is wrong with Ken this morning?" Paula asked when she came back out to the kitchen. "He sure didn't seem to be his normal, cheerful self."

"I don't know love, but I suspect that something wasn't right just by the dejected way he looked sitting and talking at the table. I hope that I really was able to help him a little."

Ken drove into the terminal parking area five minutes before the 10:00 a.m. sailing, parked the car out of the way of the boarding traffic, then ran down the ramp and onto the ferry just barely dodging the cars coming along behind him.

"Gus," he said to the day shift mate on duty, "I've got to talk to you for a minute even if it delays the sailing a little." Gus gestured to one of the seaman on deck to take over the loading for him and then picked up the sound powered telephone to call the wheelhouse.

"Captain, Ken needs to talk to me for a minute before we sail, is that okay?"

"Yes, if it's an official business discussion and not about the hockey game tonight. Make it fast though, because we'll be bucking the tide this trip and can't make up much time."

Gus hung up the phone and led Ken over to the bulwark out of the way of the traffic moving on deck.

"Alright, young corporal," Gus said, "What can an old man do for you today?"

Augustus Jenkins was unique in the BC Ferry System. He was a retired RCMP staff sergeant who quickly got tired of sitting around, fishing, and tending his garden after he and his wife moved to Quadra Island to enjoy the scenery and try out the quiet lifestyle. He had patiently waited until there was a vacancy for an ordinary seaman on the ferry system. He then worked and studied hard as staff sergeants tend to do, enjoying the regular shift schedule with none of the late night calls or interruptions on his days off that was part of his former life. As soon as he had enough qualifying sea time, he took the examination for his Mate's Certificate and eventually was promoted to his present job. He now enjoyed his work even more, with the intention of moving up to captain one day soon, even though loading and unloading cars and trucks on busy days sometimes reminded him of directing traffic as a junior constable. He also enjoyed teasing and sometimes even helping, the personnel assigned to the island's detachment.

"Gus. By any chance did you see a Ford Explorer with one or two men in it this morning?"

"I sure as hell did," Gus replied. "On the first trip to Campbell River this morning at 6:15 a.m., I saw the two businessmen in the SUV and it was loaded, the back end was down low with the weight of something in the back. It must have been parked in wet sand somewhere overnight too, because when they drove off the rear tires left two streaks of sand all the way down the deck. The heat from the engine room must have dried the sand in the tire treads on the trip over, and then when they moved off they left this trail on my clean deck."

"Where is the sand?" Ken asked panicking. "You didn't hose it off yet did you?"

"Take it easy, old buddy," Gus replied. "I just had it swept over to the scuppers, we'll hose down again later today. What's the problem, you look pale all of a sudden."

"Gus, I really need your help," Ken replied. "Constable John Novak is dead. Murdered overnight and buried in the sand on a beach north of Heriot Bay. And up until an hour ago, I didn't have one goddamned clue as to what, who or why. The only thing I know now is that Steve saw a gray Explorer with two business men in it come over on the 9:30 p.m. trip last night, and you saw a gray Explorer with two business men in it leave on the 6:15 a.m. trip. Plus, the fresh tire tracks that I saw leaving the beach lane and the trail of sand that you found this morning on your vehicle deck are clues. We need an evidence bag with some of that sand from the scupper."

"We need a hell of a lot more than that, Ken. You didn't call this in yet did you?"

"No. I didn't want to put it out over the air, and before I phoned in I wanted to try to get just a little bit of information."

"Good. Get up to the office and report in. Then have Air Division get a helicopter from Comox to the airport at Campbell River to take me to Nanaimo right away. I'll persuade the captain to bring the ferry back without a mate on board if you can get Steve to come down and take over my shift when it gets in. I'll come back later and do his shift tonight. If we hurry up I can get to the Departure Bay or Duke Point ferry terminal faster than that Ford can drive all the way down to Nanaimo, and I might just spot it going on board one of the trips out of there to Vancouver. I have a gut feeling that the car is from the mainland and not from Victoria, based on the license number. The trouble is, I can't remember just what the hell the number was right now. I also think I saw a car rental company sticker on the back bumper. And don't worry, I'll get us a bag of sand."

Just then, the bell on the sound-powered phone rang furiously. Gus trotted over and picked it up. "Yes sir, captain, I'll throw his ass off immediately and we'll get going," Gus said into the phone. He gestured for Ken to go ashore, and then continued, "I need to have a serious talk with you, captain. I'll be up there as soon as we clear the terminal."

Ken quickly drove the short distance up the road, parked the car, and went into the detachment office where he saw that the clerk was on duty and asked if there were any incoming calls. With the negative response gratefully acknowledged, he went into the house to find Marge. After sitting down at the kitchen table and telling her the whole story, leaving her in tears over Johnny, he walked back through the general office and into his own, carefully closing the door behind him.

"Island district, Sergeant Murphy," was the gruff answer to the incoming call on the Commanding Officers line.

"Sergeant, this is Corporal Mullett on Quadra Island. I need to talk to the superintendent right away. Is he there, or do you know where I can reach him?"

"This is Saturday morning, corporal, and you don't want to disturb the superintendent unless all hell is breaking loose. How can I help you?"

"Sergeant, it's extremely important that I speak to him in person. Is he there?"

"No, he is not here," said the Sergeant beginning to get annoyed, "but I do have his home phone number if you really want it, or you can speak to the Assistant Officer Commanding, Inspector Lee, who is here and is beginning to wonder what your problem is."

"Thank you, sergeant, I would like very much to talk to Inspector Lee," Ken replied sarcastically, "thanks for all your help."

"Inspector Lee here, what can I do for you corporal?"

"Sir," Ken began, "I have a situation here with a constable murdered overnight, buried in the sand on a beach north of here, I have one very meager lead, and retired Staff Sergeant Jenkins has agreed to follow up on it if Air Division can get him to Nanaimo right away. I need the mobile crime lab and the coroner, but I think the whole situation has to be kept very quiet if we are ever going to resolve this one."

The inspector began to question Ken in detail, gently drawing the entire story from him and trying to calm him at the same time. The enormity of the situation was just beginning to get to Ken and the inspector was painfully aware of what it felt like to lose a man on detachment. The sense of guilt and the burden of responsibility were tremendous, even though Ken realized that there was nothing he could have done to prevent it. Anger and

frustration would be next, so the inspector knew he had to get help to Ken, and very quickly at that. "Corporal, I fully agree with your approach," said Inspector Lee. "I will get Air Division moving right away and have the Officer-in-Charge of the General Investigation Section call you as soon as I can contact him. In the meantime, just stay where you are and write up your reports while everything is still fresh in your mind. I will call the superintendent and the duty officer at E Division to let them know what is going on, and will have Campbell River send over a couple of constables to handle your routine Saturday 911 calls. I agree that we need to keep this situation very quiet until we assess it thoroughly, so only landline telephones will be used to discuss any developments in this case."

"Yes sir. Thank you, sir." Ken slowly hung up the phone, profoundly relieved that he had handed over the bulk of the responsibility for the investigation to a senior officer, but also profoundly saddened and guilt ridden that something like this had happened to one of his detachment members on what had seemed to be a normally quiet fall weekend.

Six

onstable Ed Brewer, dressed in blue jeans and a tartan shirt, was gazing into the window of the toy store in the Nanaimo Mall. It was just after noon, and he had been checking out the display of stuffed animals, large plastic dump trucks, rubber balls and water pistols for over ten minutes now. He was a little uncomfortable spending so much time in front of the toy store window, but he would have been a lot more uncomfortable spending an equal amount of time in front of the windows of Victoria's Secret, where his wife was picking up a few necessities. A casual look or two while walking past the store was one thing, but he wasn't about to stand right outside the door waiting for her and he sure as hell wasn't going in with her ,not knowing which way it was safe to look. As he continued to fake his intense interest in the toys, he suddenly felt someone take a strong grip on his upper right arm.

"Come with me quietly sir," the voice behind him said, "I always recognize a potential shoplifter when I see one."

Ed whirled around, ready to tear a strip off the numbskull security guard who had grabbed him, and saw the grinning face of Sergeant Tim Campbell of Nanaimo Detachment. Tim quickly turned serious though, after he saw the amazed look on Ed's face followed by an expression of complete bewilderment.

"Ed, you're needed back at Quadra Island right away. Ken needs help, and there is an Air Division helicopter on its way to the airport to pick you up. It will transport you to Campbell River and a patrol unit will take you to the ferry."

"What the hell for?" Ed said in surprise. "They can get a dozen people from Campbell River Detachment faster than I can get there. Besides, we are still checked into the hotel and Doreen is in the store shopping."

"Ken doesn't need a dozen people Ed. He needs you for support and as soon as possible. You had better go into the store and get Doreen out. If I go in and get her wearing my uniform they really will think I've caught a shoplifter."

Ed got Doreen out of the store as quickly as he could without creating a scene that he couldn't explain in public. Sergeant Campbell then told her that Ed had to fly back to the

detachment right now and offered any help she might need in packing up and checking out of the hotel. He even offered to have the highway patrol escort her all the way to Campbell River if she didn't want to drive alone. Doreen declined the help, but really wanted to know what the big panic was all about, since their long awaited weekend off together was being completely screwed up. Tim told her honestly that he didn't know anything much, other than the fact that the AOC Island District had personally called the Nanaimo watch commander and asked that Ed be found and taken to the airport immediately. Doreen said that she didn't need help to check out, but she would take her time on the long drive back to Campbell River, stopping for a late lunch on the way. She told Ed not to expect her before eight o'clock, and hoped that he would be off duty and ready to tell her what was going on by the time she got home.

Tim and Ed saw her to the car, and then sped off in Tim's unit to the airport, lights and siren on all the way.

As Ed watched the helicopter rotors slow down and the doors slowly open, he was astounded to see Gus Jenkins hop out wearing his BC Ferries uniform. Ed went up to him and started to say something, but Gus just shook his head, ran past him, and jumped into Tim's patrol unit which promptly took off down the road. Ed stared after them for a minute and then climbed into the helicopter hoping that the pilot could give him some damn clue as to what the hell was going on here.

Seven

Pursuing his gut feeling that the car was a rental, hopefully from Vancouver International Airport, Gus stood patiently in the elevated traffic control room at the BC Ferries Duke Point Terminal, using borrowed binoculars to scan the automobiles and drivers in the many vehicles waiting in the boarding lanes for the Tsawwassen route. Sergeant Campbell had quickly dropped him off at the foot passenger's entrance to the terminal, because he didn't want a particular automobile's driver or passenger to see him, just in case that vehicle was in the process of arriving at the terminal. Tim, having been given a complete vehicle description by Gus, then went to the Departure Bay Terminal to check out vehicles boarding for Horseshoe Bay in West Vancouver. Gus had gone hastily up the stairs to the terminal manager's office to explain that he was part of some vague undercover investigation and then asked for the assistance that he needed.

In the meantime, the two plainclothes constables that would board whatever ferry the suspect's car boarded, checked in also. Gus explained what the game plan would be and sent them off to the passengers waiting room to mingle with the crowd and reinforce their image as casual late fall tourists.

❀ ❀ ❀

Pacing up and down, Gus was beginning to think that his idea had not been so great after all. He had arrived at the terminal just in time to see the 12:45 p.m. to Tsawwassen load and none of the cars that had waited to board looked anything like the gray Explorer he was looking for. He had just decided to wait for the 3:15 p.m. to Tsawwassen to leave and then give up, when he noticed the Explorer enter the terminal area. Strangely, if this was the same vehicle, it was not loaded down to the point where the back end was sagging as it had been earlier in the morning at Campbell River. Scanning the car with the binoculars though revealed the same two men in the car. So he quickly noted the license number and wrote it down. Moving further into the terminal area, the car entered the waiting line to board the ferry to Tsawwassen, which meant that they were on there way to somewhere south of Vancouver, possibly to the airport or across the border to the United States.

Gus quickly phoned the snack bar adjacent to the passenger's waiting room and asked the attendant to page Mrs. Smith. That got him in touch with one of the waiting plain-clothes people and Gus told her that the suspects were to board the 3:15 p.m. heading to Tsawwassen. One constable was to check out the vehicle while it was parked on the car deck, getting the vehicle identification number and anything else that could be found from the outside, including carefully scraping out dirt, sand or pebbles from the tire treads. The other detective was to mingle on the upper deck with the passengers and hopefully get some cell phone photographs of the car's occupants without being spotted. This meant wandering around, getting a lot of scenic photos to create the right image of a damn fool tourist with more time than brains. As Gus watched the large ferry pull away, he suddenly realized that he was very hungry and more importantly, that he had no way of getting home. So, after returning the binoculars and thanking the terminal manager for his assistance without telling him what he had done for him, Gus went the snack bar, ordered a double burger with chips, then used the phone to ask Nanaimo Detachment to send someone to pick him up and take him back to Campbell River.

Eight

I t was a beautiful Saturday morning on Vancouver Island. One of those clear, cold October days that made it seem possible to reach out and touch the tops of the snow peaked mountains that border the Island Highway. At 11:00 a.m., the sun was at the right angle to really show off the snow pack and the air surrounding the peaks sparkled in the sunlight.

Cruising along at exactly the posted speed limit, Inspector Michael Edward Hanley, RCMP, was thoroughly enjoying his weekend trip. He was in the process of carrying out a periodic inspection of the Criminal Investigation Section activities within the detachments in the Island District. This meant traveling to each unit, inspecting the files and talking to the detectives and support personnel about the progress of the various open cases. He had been in Port Alberni yesterday and had just left Qualicum Beach a half-hour ago. He judiciously used the cruise control system when traveling in his unmarked vehicle, because the last thing he wanted was a speeding ticket administered by an eager highway patrol constable who would be overjoyed at the opportunity to write up a commissioned officer.

After two false starts, Mike considered himself to be extremely fortunate in his career choice. He was doing something challenging and thoroughly enjoyable, albeit frustrating at times when some cases seemed to take forever to close. Mike had earned a Bachelor of Commerce Degree from the University of Manitoba and had worked for a large accounting firm just long enough to write the chartered accountant examination and gain assurances from his employer that he had a job for life. But after the hard work, intense studies and the excitement of obtaining his professional qualifications, he found the repetitive work incredibly monotonous.

Being single with a fair amount in savings, he applied for admission and was accepted at Osgoode Hall, the York University School of Law. Three hard working years later, he emerged with a degree in Business Law and gained an excellent position in the legal department of his previous employers' Toronto office. Being a bright and highly motivated young man, he found the work even more dull and dreary than he had previously, even though it offered a considerably better salary. Overwhelmed at the negative prospect of continuing in this career until retirement, he was inspired one day after reading an article on white collar crime, to write to the RCMP "O" Division headquarters in London, Ontario to see if they had any use for someone with his background. Before he knew what had happened to him, he had completed a battery of tests, had some serious interviews, passed a thorough physical, traveled to Regina, Saskatchewan and found himself a member of Cadet Troop Thirty-eight at "Depot" Division.

Michael Edward Hanley was dog-tired. Every muscle in his body ached and he was just barely making it through physical training. He had run for miles, done pushups, sit-ups and chin-ups by the thousands. He had endured foot drill for what seemed like years. He was a miserable failure, as his instructors never tired of reminding him. At age thirty, he was an old man while most of the others in his troop were children of nineteen and twenty in peak physical condition. As he lay on his bunk feeling dejected, some of the positives slowly began to come to the surface. He had aced applied police sciences and excelled in the Criminal Code courses, what better subjects for a lawyer? Come to think of it, he had received an "A" in every academic course. In self-defense and driving skills he was average, in firearms handling and target practice he was pretty good. During his training detachment days he was pretty well organized. As he slowly recovered from his fatigue, he began to have thoughts of dinner. Then he began to think about the real possibilities of graduation, which meant that he would not have to resume his former life of well-paid boredom. Newly motivated, life didn't seem quite so harsh after all.

Graduation day dawned bright, sunny and cold. At the appropriate time, families and visitors gathered at the parade square for the ceremony and the RCMP band was playing a prelude as people found their seats. Suddenly, the band changed to a marching tempo song and the crowd stood as the graduation march began to pass. Scarlet and gold were the colors, flags flew and Depot Division marched past the reviewing stand troop by proud troop, with the graduating troop last. The division then wheeled into parade rest formation in front of the stands, with the graduates standing in the front ranks for the ceremony. After the speeches, tears and laughter, the division was dismissed and the happy graduates joined their families and friends at a reception. Now as sworn peace officers and level three constables, the members of Troop Thirty-eight would receive postings to training detachments throughout Canada based on the needs of the service and, very occasionally, to accommodate personal preferences.

After the reception Mike reported to the Officer Commanding and, with his parents and senior officers as witnesses, was sworn in as a commissioned officer in accordance with the recently obtained Parliamentary Approval and his recruiting agreement. When it was all over, Inspector Michael Edward Hanley, RCMP, who now outranked even the sergeant major, was sorely tempted to go out and tell his drill instructors what he really thought of them and their sadistic practices. But wisdom prevailed as he realized that they had prepared the troop well for the harsh realities of detachment service. After all, most of the time they were not going to be dealing with model law-abiding citizens in the course of their duties.

The next day, after all of the visitors had left and the majority of his team members had gone, Mike was told to pack his uniforms and kit for storage. He was then given a plane ticket and orders to report in civilian clothing to the next Undercover Training Course to be held in Montreal.

Nine

It was Saturday morning and Michael E. Harris had just signed the lease agreement and been escorted to his studio apartment. Still holding his keys in his hand, he looked out the tenth-floor window of this new building on Denman Street not far from Stanley Park in Vancouver. From here, he could easily commute on the Davie Street trolley bus to Burrard and the high-rise office building where his new employer was located. Having applied by mail from Toronto and after several telephone interviews with various supervisors and managers, he had been offered a position as a senior accountant with the South American Shipping and Transportation Company. This company owned and operated over a dozen foreign flag ships in the export trade business from Chile, Ecuador and Peru to Asia and the west coast of Canada and the United States. Having enjoyed the view from his window overlooking English Bay for a few minutes, he sat at the kitchen table and opened the brown envelope, which he had been given before leaving Toronto. As he examined the contents, he noted the BC driver's license, social insurance card, college transcripts and an updated resume, all of which he would need when he started his new job on Monday morning. All he had to do was to remember that he was Michael E. Harris, and not the late Michael E. Hanley. He also had to memorize his

40

contact telephone number and then destroy the card that it was written on.

Monday morning was bright and pleasant as he walked the block from the bus stop to the building entrance. As he went into the elevator lobby, he noticed the young woman that had walked in ahead of him. Strikingly attractive, she waited patiently for the elevator as he gazed at her long brown hair and noted with interest that her business suit did nothing to conceal her neatly proportioned figure. Startled by the elevator bell as it arrived at the lobby level, he realized that she was frowning at him as he stood staring at her. He looked away and developed a fascination for the building directory until he realized that the elevator doors were closing. He quickly stuck his briefcase between the elevator doors to keep them from closing, then sheepishly jumped in, well aware that he had annoyed the other passengers who were anxious to get to their offices on the upper floors. Fortunately the object of his admiration had pushed the button for the eighth floor, since he had completely forgotten that he needed to get off at the human resources department for his new employee indoctrination session.

Sitting around the conference room table were ten new employees, nervously waiting for the beginning of a long morning session in which the workings of the company would be explained, numerous employment forms filled out and details provided on how each person was expected to contribute to the company bottom line. As the human resources manager cheerfully introduced herself, Mike was overjoyed to note that the object of his earlier interest was seated on the other side of the table. Each person at the table had to introduce him or herself and give a brief summary of one's educational background, family status and career interests. Mike stumbled through his academic qualifications and glossed over his dull but professional career to date, offering virtually nothing on his family background and personal details other than the fact that he was single and new in town.

As the introductions continued around the table, he learned that Susan Elizabeth Campanela was a graduate of Simon Fraser University, lived with her parents in West Vancouver and was starting her career as a buyer in the purchasing department on the sixth floor. Mike thought her voice was that of an angel and that she was even more beautiful than he had realized when he first saw her. Unfortunately, he was also staring at her again and got another dirty look for his trouble. This also seemed to prompt the manager to begin the lecture on the swift punishment that would occur if any incidents of discrimination or sexual harassment were reported.

During the coffee break, Mike managed to make his way over to the corner where Susan was chatting with another young woman. When the woman moved away to get more coffee, Mike introduced himself again and asked Susan if she would like to join him for lunch, since he was new in the area and not familiar with the restaurants near by. With an icy stare, Ms. Campanela reminded Mr. Harris that lunch was going to be provided to all new employees in the company cafeteria as part of their tour of the facilities, including their introduction to the various departmental locations throughout the building. She then moved away to get more coffee for herself. The afternoon tour concluded with a visit to one of the companies' ships, which coincidentally happened to be at Ballentyne Pier that afternoon. The ship was topping off its cargo prior to sailing to Chile that evening and the *Gran Peruvian* was bustling with activity as the stevedores completed their loading activities and started securing the cargo cranes for sea.

Mike had been impressed with the overall size of the company operation during their departmental tour and was beginning to realize how many people it took to run an organization with ships operating all over the world. Even the marketing activity involved in securing cargo consolidation contracts to keep the ships profitably employed required large numbers of people working two shifts on the telephones to cover the many different time zones in which the organization traded. In fact, that very profitable employment was his reason for joining the firm. While the ships that operated exclusively between various foreign ports and never came to Canada were immensely profitable according to the financial statements, the ships trading to and from Canada never had made a profit, and thus had never paid any corporate income taxes. Since foreign registered ships that were operated by a company with headquarters in Canada but traded exclusively elsewhere were not subject to Canadian taxes, only the ships regularly serving Vancouver and the other West Coast ports were potential federal revenue sources. And it was these ships that never made a profit for some strange reason, even though they provided regular weekly liner service to and from South America.

Mike reported to the accounts receivable department on the fifth floor at 8:00 a.m. on Tuesday morning to begin his regular work. His manager seemed relieved that Mike had no previous shipping company experience in his background and emphasized the fact that Mike was to follow only the strict company guidelines in performing his auditing tasks. He was not to be innovative in any way. If he worked hard, got along well with the other employees and his supervisors, he could expect to have a lucrative career. But he was not to question any successful company business practices, since the shipping company board of directors was very conservative and didn't like anyone who made waves. After recovering from the forced laughter at his seemingly humorous remark, the manager then showed Mike to his tiny office and gave him some perfunctory instructions on operating the computer and gaining access to the necessary data files. On his way out, he remembered that he had not introduced Mike to anyone else on the floor, so he quickly took him around to meet the other accountants working nearby.

As he began to get a feel for the work routine and what was expected of him, Mike gradually stayed a little later each day so that he had some time on the computer during the second shift after the others in his department had gone home. He quickly discovered that he had limited access to the financial files associated with accounts receivable and no access whatever dealing with accounts payable, ship operations, or the purchasing department files. He had access to the customer accounts and the invoicing activity, so he knew that the revenues were substantial each week, but he had no idea of what the total operations were costing the company.

Leaving late one Tuesday evening, Mike pushed the button for the elevator which came down quickly from the floor above. As the door opened, he was pleasantly surprised to see Susan on the elevator by herself. He very politely said, "Hello," and asked how she was doing with her new job. Equally surprising was her pleasant response and apology for being short with him on that first day. She explained that she had been nervous about starting her first full time job and wanted to be sure that she was doing everything correctly from the beginning. She also said that her boss was really good to work for and she was learning a lot as she got into the routine of dealing with the various suppliers.

"Well," said Mike, "if you really are sorry for me, I'll renew my invitation. Let's have lunch together tomorrow."

Susan thought about it for a minute or so, just long enough for Mike to think that she was going to say "No."

"Alright, I must admit that I really would like to," she said. "But we'll have to eat in the cafeteria because I don't know much about the restaurants around here either. I do know that we would never be able to go outside to eat and then be back in an hour. My boss is good, but he has said something to other women who were late getting back after lunch." Mike agreed quickly, and they planned to meet outside the cafeteria at five past twelve the next day.

Waiting across from the elevators on the cafeteria level, Mike was just about convinced that she wasn't coming. It was about 12:15 p.m., and the cafeteria waiting line was now very short and most of the seats were taken. Mike had just decided to go in alone when a bell chimed and an elevator arrived at the floor. Susan rushed out and over to him apologetically, explaining that she had been on the phone with a supplier who wouldn't stop talking long enough for her to say that she just had to go. She looked so nice in her spring dress that Mike would have forgiven her for just about anything. Without thinking, he took her gently by the arm and steered her into the cafeteria. Fortunately, she didn't object, handed him a tray, and began making selections for both of them. They found the last empty table and sat down.

Susan began to eat and then suddenly stopped and leaned towards Mike, who hadn't picked up his fork. "Michael Harris, if you don't stop staring at my chest and eat something, you are going to be all alone and very hungry by one o'clock."

"I'm sorry, I didn't mean to do it again," Mike said. "But you're so beautiful that I don't even know what's on my tray. Your eyes, your hair, everything about you is special. But I really don't want you to be mad at me, so I'll eat whatever it is that I've got here and pay no attention to you at all."

She laughed gently and said, "I really think you mean it, so I won't get mad at you this time. But if I find out that this is the line that you give to all the girls, I won't be so forgiving next time."

They spent the next thirty-five minutes exchanging stories of childhood. Mike describing growing up in Winnipeg with snowy, fifty degree below zero winters and learning to play hockey at the neighborhood rink. Susan talked about trips to Stanley Park and ferry rides to Bowen Island in the summer. Before they knew it, it was time to go and they hurried over to the elevators. As they stood waiting, Mike worked up his courage. "Susan, if I promise not to stare at you too much, will you have dinner with me on Saturday evening?"

"Well, I really should check my busy social calendar first," Susan replied, "but if you come and get me in a nice car and let me choose the restaurant, I'll seriously consider it." They got on the elevator, Mike forgot to push any of the buttons, so they headed to Susan's floor.

"I just realized," Mike blurted, "I don't have a car. I just moved here a couple of weeks ago. But I will get one before Saturday night. What kind would you like?"

Susan laughed again. "You don't have to get one just to take me out," she said, "but if you do, get something red and sporty looking." Then she got off the elevator and moved down the hall to work, leaving Mike to figure out how to get to his floor and into his office on time.

On Thursday morning, Mike picked up his phone and dialed an inside number.

"Purchasing department, Susan Campanela speaking," was the business-like response.

"Michael Harris, accounts receivable," was the equally formal reply. "Susan, I forgot to ask you where you live and how to find you," Mike said somewhat breathlessly. "Could you give me some directions and tell me what time to pick you up?"

"Yes sir," was the reply, "but I will have to call you back in a few minutes. Please give me a number where I can reach you."

Mike, realized that the boss must be nearby, formally gave her his work number and said, "Good-bye." Ten minutes later his phone rang.

"Well, Mr. Harris, so you don't know where to find me?" Susan said, "How will I ever see your new car?"

"I have a better idea," Mike said, "why don't you come with me to help pick it out on Saturday morning? We can go to a dealer near your place if you like."

They agreed that Susan would meet him at the Sea Bus terminal in North Vancouver at 11:00 a.m., then they would go to a few of the nearby dealers to see what they had available for immediate delivery. She also offered to take him to the dealership where she got her old Buick if he was interested.

On the way home from the bus stop that evening, Mike stopped at a payphone and dialed a number from memory. He waited for the reply and then explained that he had an urgent problem. "I want to buy an automobile on Saturday morning," Mike said. "But I realized that Michael Harris has no credit history at all." There was a long pause, then a somewhat obscene exclamation and then another long pause.

"You would think of something like that on a Thursday evening when you need a car on Saturday morning. I suppose you have a hot date and want to seem like a normal human being for a change?"

"Yes, it's something like that," Mike confessed.

"OK, call me again at this time tomorrow and I'll tell you

where you can get financing without answering a lot of questions. I'll also have to arrange for insurance, since you have no driving record either."

"Hey, thanks a lot," Mike replied. "I have a work related request also. Could I have a PC and modem installed in my apartment with some sort of connection to my office network? I just can't get enough privacy at work to dig into the files the way I would like to, and they get suspicious if I hang around late every night."

"That can be done. No date for you tomorrow night though, Romeo, some people will be over around seven to get you set up with a system."

"Thanks again. I knew I could count on the efficiency of the Force to meet my every little wish."

"And to hell with you too," was the reply. "Have a good night."

Promptly at 7:00 p.m. on Friday, the intercom buzzer in the apartment sounded. Mike pushed the button to release the front door and went out into the hall in front of his apartment. A couple of minutes later two men wearing the coveralls of a popular Vancouver electronics retailer got off the elevator, each pushing a handcart loaded with a number of IBM boxes. After Mike ushered them in and closed the door, the older of the two introduced himself to Mike.

"Sergeant Foster, sir," he said, "and this is Constable Chang. We have your computer system here. Just give us a little while to get you set up and then the constable will give you some instructions on accessing your office files without upsetting their security system. If you get caught of course, you are on your own. We don't know you at all."

An hour later Mike had a functioning system, several instruction books, and lots of notes that he had taken as Constable Chang very patiently described his network access instructions. Most importantly, he was only to connect during a normal day time or evening office-work shift since the home computer carried the same identification as the one he used at work. The company security network would identify it as one of their own. Mike was not to try anything until Monday, since the two men would go to his office building in a TELUS telephone company truck over the weekend to check out some reported line connection problems in the telephone equipment room.

Ten

I t was breezy on the water, but the trip across Vancouver Harbor was incredibly scenic on this sunny Saturday morning. Many ships at anchor to look at and the mountains were crystal clear as the Sea Bus approached the North Shore. As the vessel slowed to enter the terminal, Mike could see Susan waiting beside her car. He rushed off the Sea Bus and went up the ramp to the street where she was parked.

"Good morning," Mike said. "You look extra lovely on this sunny Saturday morning, I'm really glad you agreed to this adventure."

"The agreement only lasts until you start staring at me again," Susan replied. "I'm still trying to decide if you keep looking at my face or my figure."

"How about a little of both," Mike replied. "They're both sensational."

"Enough of that," Susan said laughingly, "get in the car and we'll drive up to auto row where the car dealers are close together. Then we'll see if you are a serious buyer or not."

The next two hours went by quickly as they looked at rows of new cars, took test drives in two of them, and began to realize how hungry they were. They excused themselves from the most persistent of the salesmen and promised to return soon. Then

Susan drove them back down to the waterfront where they found a quiet restaurant for lunch. Susan offered to pay for lunch if their dinner date was still on, since Mike hadn't asked her out for two consecutive meals and she was looking forward to dinner at the restaurant where she had made the reservations for the evening. Mike said that he would cheerfully pay for both if the bill wasn't too much more than the value of the gasoline that she was using to drive them around car hunting. With these important ground rules established, they enjoyed their time together over lunch so much so that they almost forgot what they were in North Vancouver to do.

At three o'clock they drove to the dealer where Susan's father had bought her car when she started to commute to the university. Once again they first looked at the rows of new cars outside that were available, and finally went into the show room where they were immediately attracted to the centerpiece on the floor. A loaded bright red Buick Lacrosse, with the optional hybrid assist engine. Mike immediately decided that this was it. He and Susan sat in the car, tried the radio and electric windows, then checked out the trunk and lifted the hood. This naturally attracted the closest salesman, but Susan asked for the man who had been the salesman when her father bought her car. It turned out that he had just returned to his desk from processing another sale, but he still greeted them enthusiastically. He became a little more reserved when Mike asked if the car that they had selected could be delivered that afternoon. He said that he would ask the sales manager but he was pretty sure that it could not be done, even if they were to agree on the price and financing terms. As the salesman went off, Susan became concerned.

"Mike, please don't feel obliged to spend a lot of money just because I said I liked a nice car," she said seriously. "This is expensive and I don't want to be responsible for your going into debt because of a feeling that you have to impress me."

Mike laughed gently and said, "Susan, I've been wanting a car of my own ever since I started working at my first job after college, but I never had a need for one before. The public transportation system in Toronto is excellent. When I was in law school I didn't have time to drive anywhere even if I wanted to and when I was working downtown I could walk to work from my apartment. Here in the Vancouver area I need a car, especially if you let me see you occasionally and you're living half way up a mountain someplace."

Just then the salesman returned and apologetically said that the car could not possibly be ready for delivery before Tuesday, but if he would like to fill out a sales agreement and leave a deposit then they could at least get the process started. Mike said that he would sign a sales agreement for ten percent off the sticker price and write a check for half the amount right now if the car was ready by five o'clock. The salesman said that he would get the sales manager.

The manager came bustling up and shook Mike's hand. Ignoring Susan, he said that he would like to help but there was no way he could get approval for financing the vehicle until Monday. Mike, starting to get a little annoyed, suggested that he call his bank right now to determine if he wasn't already approved. The manager then painstakingly wrote down Mike's full name, address, bank details and place of employment and sarcastically said that he would see what he could do.

He came back in five minutes and politely said, "Mr. Harris, your loan is fully approved. I don't know how or why. If you sit down with the salesman and fill out all of the necessary paperwork I will get the car serviced and ready for delivery by our six o'clock, closing time." As the form preparation was completed, the check written and the car carefully driven off the showroom floor and over to the new car service center, Mike and Susan were ushered out and told to return just before six. It was after four o'clock and their dinner reservation was for seven. Susan said that she had to get home to get ready but she couldn't let Mike just hang around the streets for two hours. So she said that if he promised to behave and didn't read too much into it, she would take him home to meet her mother so that he could wait there in comfort. They went along Marine Drive, continued into West Vancouver, and then turned up into the British Properties area. Mike was enjoying the scenery as they climbed higher and was becoming very impressed with both the view and the fine homes they were passing. Finally, Susan turned into the driveway of a magnificent ranch style home on what looked to be five acres or more, with a superb view of the Straits far below.

"Who do you know that lives in a palace like this?" Mike asked in amazement.

"My mother and father," replied Susan. "They let me live here too."

"I'm really sorry Susan, I think I've made a mistake," Mike said. "I'm just a plain old prairie boy. I've never been in a house like this in my life. Just take me back to a bus stop and I won't bother you any more."

"Don't be silly," Susan said laughing. "You're a chartered accountant, have a law degree and hold down a very good job. I'm sure you are qualified to at least meet my mother. Besides, I'll protect you from any major social blunders. After all, it is Saturday afternoon and formal dress is definitely not required."

Susan parked her car in the driveway in front of the garage doors and pushed the button on the remote control on the sun visor. One of the four doors opened and they got out of the car and entered the kitchen through the garage. Mike couldn't help but notice the two Cadillac sedans parked side by side as they walked past and naturally wondered what kind of car normally occupied the space next to the one where Susan obviously parked hers regularly.

"Hello, I'm Liz Campanela," the radiant woman in the sun dress said as she held out her hand to Mike, "Susan has told me about you and I'm very pleased to meet you. I see that she was right about you staring at people occasionally."

"Very pleased to meet you, Mrs. Campanela," Mike stammered. "I really don't stare normally, but you do look remarkably like your daughter."

"Quick thinking, Michael," Susan said. "Now come on out and sit on the porch and I'm sure that mother will find you something to drink while I get changed."

Mike sat down at the patio table and gratefully accepted a frosted mug of root beer. Susan's mother said that she would have offered him something stronger, but she knew that he would be taking delivery of his new car soon and shouldn't have liquor on his breath when he did so. Mike was impressed with her understanding and acceptance of him and told her that. She in turn explained that Susan rarely, if ever, brought someone home to meet her parents, so she concluded that he must be at least a little bit special. Besides, Susan had been chattering all last evening about this car buying adventure and the dinner date that she was looking forward to. Mrs. Campanela also explained that her husband was at the club playing golf, but might be home before they left. In any event, one of them would take them to the dealer so that Susan's car could be left at home.

As they continued their conversation, Liz casually drew Mike out about his background, education, parents and lifestyle, as any good mother would when considering a young man that her daughter seemed interested in. Mike, while not wanting to hold anything back, had to be extremely careful not to reveal what his real job was. He was now getting very concerned about how to handle things when the time came to close out the case. Susan came in at that point and Mike stared at her breasts again. He just couldn't help it, Susan was so lovely in the semi-formal dress, which was more than suitable for dining and dancing in any elegant hotel ballroom.

"Whoa," Mike said. "Wherever it is we're going, I'm obviously not dressed for it. Should I go home and change after we pick up the car?"

"No, you'll do. People will just think I picked up a scruffy tourist someplace. It actually gets cool up on the mountain late in the evening, so I chose something that I can wear with a sweater to keep me warm. Get up on your feet and mother will take us to the car dealer."

They had just pulled onto the road from the driveway when a blue Corvette convertible, top down, came up the hill. A handsome man wearing a golf shirt and plaid cap flagged them down and stopped his car beside them. Introductions were made and Susan's father made Mike promise to bring the new car back tomorrow afternoon so that he could test-drive it. Naturally, he would be expected to stay for dinner. Then the Corvette moved into the driveway while they continued on down the road.

The car was gleaming in the sun, ready to go as promised. Susan's mother inspected it with approval and watched Mike gingerly get in while the salesman explained where every thing was, light switches, horn, stereo controls and start button. Mike then started the car, got out, and waved Susan into the driver's sea. "You know how to get to the restaurant, please take the wheel and get us there."

"But it's your new car," Susan protested while quickly getting into the driver's seat. "You're right though, I do know the fastest way to get there. Wave 'good bye' to mother and hop in."

Liz Campanela smiled, shook her head and waved as Mike and Susan headed out onto Marine Drive, concluding that they really did make a striking couple. Susan cautiously moved along to Capilano Road and then headed up the hill to the Grouse Mountain resort parking lot. They rode the gondola lift up the side of the mountain and Mike marveled at the view, amazed at how high they actually were as they reached the top of the lift. The view of Vancouver Harbor, Stanley Park and out across the Straits was so breathtaking from the restaurant that Susan just quietly watched, as Mike, not being used to scenery like this, took it all in. After a long pleasant evening of drinks, dinner, and easy conversation they finally headed back down the mountain and reluctantly began the slow drive back to West Vancouver and Susan's home. Mike walked her to the front door, said goodnight, and leaned forward to kiss her cheek. She turned, gave him a long, lingering kiss, and then ran inside leaving him standing there stunned at his good fortune. New car and newly in love with a wonderful girl and not the slightest idea how to find his way back to his apartment in Vancouver.

Eleven

Mike was spending long hours on his computer each weekday evening. He was gradually getting beyond the password checkpoints and into the files of many of the other departments. Occasionally he had to call Constable Chang for advice, but he was really making progress and learning a great deal about company financial operations.

Weekends were a different story. Having lunch with Susan in the cafeteria almost every working day, dinners together in a lively downtown restaurant on Fridays and quiet country inn dinners on Saturdays were now the normal routine. Most Sundays now meant going to the late morning Mass with Susan and her parents in their parish church, followed by brunch either at the Campanela home or in a West Vancouver restaurant, then a drive or a ferry excursion for a relaxing afternoon together. It was getting very hard for Mike to concentrate on his primary mission in life, catching white-collar criminals.

One Monday evening, after an especially wonderful weekend with Susan, Mike was deep into the marine operations department files and found something very interesting. The ships that were operating on the South American service from the west coast of Canada and the United States were just as profitable as the ships trading between ports in Europe or Asia, but had incredibly bad luck near the end of each fiscal year. Very expensive shipyard repairs correcting problems such as seized main engine bearings, broken propeller shafts, generator engine crankcase explosions, cracked cylinder heads, hull plating replacements due to both grounding and cargo hold wastage seemed to occur on each ship each year. The repair work was always done in shipyards located in Ecuador, Peru or Chile. Seemingly, the bad luck never struck on the North American leg of the voyages.

The ship repairs were always performed in conjunction with the annual dry dock and survey periods, and greatly prolonged the time spent in the shipyards, which charged highly inflated daily rates. Mike excitedly searched the historical records as far back as he could go and found the same pattern. Ships assigned to the European-Mediterranean and the Asian-Australian services had normal repair costs and were profitable each year. Those assigned to the taxable North American routes were not. Obtaining proof of fraud that would stand up in court was now the problem.

During lunch the next day, Mike casually asked Susan if the purchasing department always required competitive bids for purchases and services.

"Yes always," Susan replied. "They're very particular about having at least three bids for all purchase orders issued. The only exceptions are the long-term contracts for voyage repairs performed in shipyards in the south and for the fuel oil and ship's stores delivered in Vancouver. But everything else purchased requires quotations that have been obtained in advance. The real question is what does any of that have to do with planning our adventures this weekend?"

Mike, lost in thought, didn't reply immediately so Susan gently kicked him under the table. "Hey, are you staying up too late with that computer of yours or am I boring you?"

"Sorry, I was trying to get up enough courage to ask you to spend the weekend in Victoria with me and do some sightseeing on the island. We would have separate rooms at the Empress of course."

"That would be wonderful," Susan said excitedly. "I love Victoria, the shopping on Government Street, the museums, and parking on Dallas Road to see the ships head out to sea. Let's go over there early on Saturday morning and come back Sunday night. I'll tell mother that we're going and make the reservations this afternoon."

Twelve

I t was gray and drizzling on Wednesday morning as the three men walked down the pier towards the *Gran Chilean* at Lynn Terminal. The ship had just completed loading cargo and the stevedores were securing the hatches as the crew busily loaded groceries aft. Using the stores crane, they were lifting the small aluminum containers unloaded by the Quality Hotel and Restaurant Supply Company truck from the pier to the deck area just aft of the superstructure. The three climbed up the accommodation ladder to the main deck and presented their identity cards to the watchman, requesting that the captain be called. The chief officer soon appeared demanding to know what they wanted, since the ship was preparing to sail in two hours.

Once again identification cards were produced, and Captain Jack McLennan explained that they were all from the Marine Inspection Service of the Transport Ministry and were going to conduct a Port State Inspection prior to the vessel being allowed to leave the harbor. Under international law, even though the ship did not fly the Canadian flag, a safety inspection could be conducted by the National Authorities to ensure that the requirements of the International Maritime Organization had been complied with. The chief officer was not at all impressed and insisted that they wait while he conferred with the captain.

That worthy soon appeared with the chief engineer in tow, and loudly proclaimed that his ship was in perfect condition, no grievances had been filed by the crew and all his paperwork was in order. He then told them to leave his ship.

Captain McLennan explained to the captain that no pilot would appear, nor would docking tugs come alongside to assist the ship's departure until the inspection was satisfactorily completed. He told the captain that he personally would inspect the ship's navigating bridge and logbooks, Mr. Colin McPherson would accompany the chief engineer to inspect the main engine and auxiliary machinery and Mr. Matthews would accompany the chief officer to inspect the cargo gear, lifeboats and the fire fighting equipment. He then ordered the captain to lead the way to the bridge.

Colin McPherson, Staff Sergeant, Marine Section RCMP "E" Division, now nominally a Transport Canada Marine Inspector, stepped from the elevator into the machinery control room. He immediately complimented the chief engineer for the clean, well-kept environment in which all of the control console equipment and computer monitors seemed to be in perfect working order. The engineer on watch greeted them and asked how he could assist them. Colin asked to see the engine room log book and the oil discharge record book before he began his inspection of the machinery spaces themselves. The chief happily produced them and invited Colin to take as much time as necessary for his examination. Colin, seemingly as an afterthought, also asked for the engineer's maintenance workbook.

As Colin and the chief engineer slowly made their way around the immaculate and well-maintained main engine, Colin casually asked about the four cracked cylinder liners that had to be replaced last February. The chief stopped and looked at him in amazement.

"Carumba! There have never been repairs like that on this engine," he replied. "Where did you get an idea like that?"

"Well," said Colin, "what about the crankcase explosion on Number Two Generator set?' "You must be loco," said the chief. "Why are you saying such things when you can see the good condition of my machinery?"

Colin apologized and readily admitted that the Inspection Service must have been confused about which ship was to be inspected. He once again complimented the chief on his propulsion plant, and said that if he could get copies of the engine room log and workbook entries for the last year, he would correct the official inspection records the very next day. The chief led him back to the control room and immediately sent the watch engineer to the engineering department office to copy the logs. He then poured coffee for Colin and himself and described his practice of continuous preventive maintenance to keep the machinery in first class condition and to reduce the cost of the annual shipyard repairs. Colin once more commented that it was a pleasure to see a plant maintained in such good condition and that his report would reflect very favorably on the *Gran Chilean* engineering department.

Captain McLennan had a virtually identical experience on the bridge, receiving vehement denials and the production of logbook records when he asked about the ship running aground and the subsequent replacement of bottom shell plating during a shipyard dry dock period. Once again apologies were offered with the admission that the Marine Inspection Service was obviously in error about which ship really required an inspection.

Martin Matthews, having completed his inspection rounds with the chief officer and finding everything in good order, was casually watching the operation of the stores crane as the supplies were loaded. His interest picked up when four green army duffel bags were taken from the rear door of the truck, loaded onto a pallet, and hoisted on board. The bags were full, but must have been fairly light, since the crane hoisted them at a higher speed than that required for the containers. The purser immediately claimed them as they arrived on board, and ordered the seamen to take them to his office at once. *Strange,* thought Martin, *what is the grocery truck doing delivering things like that? And what in the world does the purser want with scruffy looking duffel bags?* He made a mental note to tell Captain McLennan about it in his report.

On Thursday evening, at 657 West Thirty-seventh Avenue, the "E" Division General Investigation Section conference room lights were burning brightly much later than usual. Chief Superintendent Singh, Inspector Janice Marshall of the White Collar Crimes unit, and Staff Sergeant Colin McPherson were huddled around the table comparing ship log book records with detailed voyage repair cost data. These and other computerized financial records had been surreptitiously passed from Mike Harris to a plainclothes constable in Stanley Park. The comparison data was far better than anyone had expected. For each ship on the money losing North American service, the payments for shipyard work performed bore no resemblance to the ship's records of work needed. In addition, the

Classification Society Survey reports confirmed the ship's records. It was becoming obvious that this was a tax evasion or money laundering conspiracy at the very highest levels in the South American Shipping and Transportation Company. Each operating division seemed to be functioning properly, but the financial information was so compartmentalized that the management of one department had absolutely no knowledge of how another was performing. The meeting closed with the consensus that there was now sufficient evidence to get the Attorney General's office involved, and that Mike Harris should end his short financial career with the company.

Thirteen

Saturday morning dawned bright and beautiful. As Mike and Susan cruised along the Upper Levels Highway to the ferry terminal at Horseshoe Bay, Mike was deep in thought. He now had a great deal more to talk to Susan about during their weekend adventure in Victoria than he had originally planned on. He knew that timing was everything, but had no concept of what order he should do things. Susan was really excited about their weekend plans, maybe even half expecting that Mike was going to pop THE question. That is what he intended to do of course, particularly since he had the ring with him, but now he had much more to tell her, including revealing his true identity and letting her know that he had given two weeks notice to his boss last night.

Susan brought him back to reality as they approached the booth to buy the ferry tickets. She suggested that as soon as they got on board for the trip to Nanaimo that they get into the cafeteria line for breakfast and enjoy the scenery while they eat. Mike agreed and decided to delay any serious conversation until later that evening, after what would hopefully be a fun-filled day on the island. Susan began to notice a subtle change in Mike as they drove south on the Island Highway towards Victoria. Even though the Lacrosse had plenty of power to charge up and down the hills on the way, ninety percent of the traffic was passing them as Mike precisely maintained the speed limit.

"Hey, old man," she said, "do you want a real driver to take over so that we can get there sometime today?"

"Come on," Mike replied. "You know I have this phobia about getting a speeding ticket, this car always looks as though it's going faster than it really is."

"Sure, but in this case everyone else is passing us, so they're obviously not part of the illusion."

Mike increased speed to that of the traffic flow and Susan leaned back contentedly in her seat and turned up the radio. They made good time over the Malahat section of the highway and were going past Goldstream Park on the final approach to Victoria when Mike's worst fear occurred. A highway patrol car with blue and red lights flashing came up behind them and waved them over to the side of the road. Mike pulled over, gave Susan a dirty look, rolled down the window, and sat with both hands on top of the steering wheel waiting for the constable to approach him. After what seemed like forever, because of the computer check of the license number, the constable appeared.

"You know that you were exceeding the posted speed limit?"

"Yes, but I was just following the flow of traffic so as not to create a bottleneck."

"Good excuse, but they all use it. Is this your automobile?"

"Yes it is. I bought it two months ago."

"May I have your driver's license, registration and insurance card please?"

Mike dutifully pulled them out of his wallet and the glove compartment and handed them over. The constable then went back to his car and got on the radio, once again taking a very long time. Susan was getting really concerned by this time. This was not typical of any other traffic stop that she had experienced while driving with her parents. She glanced at Mike and saw him with his hands still on top of the steering wheel, looking straight-ahead and very annoyed. Finally, the constable returned and handed Mike his documents.

"I have a message from the Island District Watch Commander for you, sir."

"What would that be constable?"

"In the future, watch your ass, sir."

"Thank you constable, I most certainly will."

At that, the constable returned to his cruiser and pulled away, leaving Susan more puzzled than ever. "What in the world was that all about? You didn't get a ticket, and that was the strangest warning message that I've ever heard from a policeman!"

"Well," Mike replied, "that is just one more thing that I have to explain to you this weekend. But since we're so close to Victoria and I don't know my way around, how about your driving the rest of the way and for God's sake watch the speed limit."

After maneuvering into the parking garage behind the hotel, they checked into the Empress, getting rooms three floors apart much to Mike's disgust. They then shopped Government Street until Mike couldn't stand another store. Susan finally took pity on him and they took the horse drawn Tally-Ho ride through Beacon Hill Park so that Mike could relax and enjoy the scenery while Susan looked through her shopping treasures.

That evening, after a long leisurely dinner at the Oak Bay Marina, Mike began the slow drive back to the Empress by the scenic waterfront route and parked in the Beacon Hill lot which overlooked the Straits of Juan de Fuca and the twinkling lights of

Port Angeles, Washington, twenty miles away. Susan snuggled up beside him and they enjoyed the peaceful scene in front of them, kissing periodically to keep up with their neighbors in adjacent cars, since that seemed to be the local custom. As the evening wore on, the moonlight began to sparkle on the wave tops in front of them and Mike knew that the time had come. But what order should he approach things without creating a disaster out of an almost perfect weekend trip?

"Susan," Mike said gently after a long drawn out kiss, "will you marry me?"

"Oh Mike, I was so hoping that you would ask me tonight, it's been such a wonderful day and I love you so very much."

"I just happen to have a ring that I picked up somewhere along the way and it might just fit," Mike said. "Would you like to try it on? I also have a few family secrets to tell you about that might make you change your mind about keeping it." Mike made a big production of fishing through his pockets and finally pulled out a ring box. As Mike opened it, Susan could see the diamond gleaming in the moonlight and held out her hand so that Mike could slip it on her finger. It fit perfectly, since Mike had done a little detective work quite awhile ago and somehow got her ring size from her mother without letting on why he wanted to know. Liz, of course, had gone along with his request maintaining the pretense that she had no idea of what was going on.

They continued to cuddle and kiss as Susan stole occasional glances at the ring. Mike unbuttoned her blouse and Susan removed her bra so that Mike finally had the opportunity to caress the beautiful breasts that he had admired for so long. It was getting very late so they reluctantly agreed that it was really time to go. When Susan had slowly dressed and become presentable once again, Mike cleared his throat, sat up straight and announced that it was time for a very serious talk. He then told her his life story all over again, pointing out the differences from what he had told her before, and swearing her to secrecy about his real job at their office. She drew away from him, looking at him in amazement as she comprehended that his name was Hanley, not Harris, and that he was an undercover inspector in the RCMP. She began to weep softly as she realized that her perfect world was not quite what she had imagined it to be. Then as Mike, terrified of losing her, earnestly reassured her of his love and reminded her of all the things about him that were the same, she began to realize that maybe things weren't so very different after all.

They got back to the hotel at 3:00 a.m., and after agreeing to meet in the lobby at 10:00 a.m., went their separate ways to bed. Mike was overjoyed to realize that Susan had kept the ring and managed to sleep very well. Too well, as he realized when the phone beside him began to chime and the bedside clock indicated 10:15 a.m.

"Good morning," Susan said cheerfully, "I thought there was a promise of breakfast with this tour. Think you can manage to meet me in the coffee shop sometime soon?" "I'll shave, shower and be there in record time. Order whatever is good with lots of coffee. Do we still have a lot of planning to do together?"

"More than ever before. I phoned mom and dad to tell them about the ring. I didn't tell them about anything else though, I think that we had better do that together."

Fourteen

"Courtenay, Courtenay 3. Land line immediate."

The radio call had rudely interrupted Mike Hanley's pleasant daydreams as he cruised along the highway in the late morning sunshine. He reached for his microphone:

"Courtenay 3, Courtenay. 10-4, on my way."

He reached down and flipped on the lights and siren as he picked up speed to get to the payphone at the service station at Union Bay, just a few miles up the road. He pulled into the parking lot, shut down the car, and sprinted over to the phone ignoring the stares from the locals and thankful that no one else was using it. Calling 911, he identified himself and asked to be transferred to whoever had called for him.

"Ed Lee here, Mike. A constable has been murdered on Quadra Island and there are very few details so far. The NCOIC-of the detachment, Corporal Mullet, is in his office waiting for you to call. I've told the superintendent and the district duty officer. Corporal Mullet seems to think that this should be kept away from the press for now, so we're only using landlines for communication. I've called in your staff sergeant so he should be available in your office any time now. Good luck on this one, call if I can do anything else from here."

"Thanks, Ed. I'll call the detachment from this phone. Please ask the staff sergeant to round up the mobile crime lab crew and ask the coroner to head up to the scene. I'll keep you informed by telephone as things develop. It looks as though Susan and I won't be seeing you for dinner tonight after all. Sorry about that, we were really looking forward to our get-together." Mike then called the Quadra Island Detachment and carefully listened to the details of everything that Corporal Mullet had seen and done so far, including the good work that Gus Jenkins had started for them. He asked Mullet to explain again why he felt so strongly that no one on the island could be responsible. Listening carefully, he acknowledged that under the circumstances, no fight in the parking lot of a pub, no gathering of local drunks or malcontents near a café, but only the buried body of a constable in a very remote beach location with no 911 calls reporting a disturbance of any kind certainly indicated that something very unusual had gone down. He asked the corporal to request more help from Campbell River and then send someone to remain at the site to chase away casual visitors without letting on why. He also asked him to have someone meet the disguised crime lab vehicle with its plainclothes crew at the ferry terminal when it arrived to guide them to the scene. He indicated that he would arrive just as soon as possible, and then he hung up and dialed his own office in Courtenay.

"Criminal Investigation Section, Staff Sergeant Blake speaking."

"Hello John. I just got off the phone with Corporal Mullet and here's what we need to do. Send the mobile crime lab vehicle over to maintenance and have them spray paint over any identifying markings and then stencil Sam's Wholesale Hardware or something like it on each front door. Then make sure that the crew are all in plainclothes and send them on their way to the island. Round up some more people and have them go through every commercial trash dumpster between the scene and the ferry terminal to see what they can find. They can make up some fool story about being environmental inspectors if anyone should ask them what they are doing. Corporal Mullet can tell them where to look for the dumpsters. I'm going to stop at home to get some clean clothes and then go to the scene. Please stand by at the office to coordinate things until I call you from the island."

Mike then picked up the phone again and called home to ask Susan if she would like to spend a few days at a cozy resort on Quadra Island with him, leaving in about twenty minutes. No explanation possible until he saw her of course; and yes, he had told the Lees that they couldn't make it for dinner tonight after all. Susan, with just over one year's experience as an RCMP spouse, already knew better than to ask questions just then and graciously accepted the invitation. She also knew that she was probably needed for something and besides, if she didn't agree to go she probably wouldn't see him for at least a week anyway.

Fifteen

The vibration on the vehicle deck of a Nanaimo-Tsawwassen ferry running at full speed was very annoying when a person was sitting on the steel deck, out of sight between two cars, and trying to scrape material from tire treads into an evidence bag. Constable Kunzig had already obtained the really valuable information, the license plate number, and VIN number and, of utmost importance, the Hertz identification number from the small sticker that identified the car as a rental vehicle. Just a few minutes more of this activity and he would go and find a safe place to call in the information from his cell phone. He wondered how Constable Drake was doing in her role topside as a tourist/photographer. Finishing up, he brushed off his pants and put the bag and his notebook into his jacket pockets. He then went up the aft set of stairs to the main deck and made his way slowly forward through the various seating areas until he spotted Shirley with her camera near the forward lounge windows. He waited until she noticed him standing in the doorway and then gestured for her to come and meet him. She took a couple of final pictures in the opposite direction from the objects of interest and then slowly made her way out of the lounge.

Shirley was pleased to finish up her part of the job, since some people in the lounge were really beginning to notice and watch what she was doing, although her prize subjects had been deep in conversation and hopefully had paid no attention to her. She and Brian then went to an outside area on the upper deck and moved aft past the sign that said, *No Passengers Permitted* to an alcove where the phone could be used without too much interference. "Criminal Investigation Section, Staff Sergeant Blake speaking."

"Good afternoon staff sergeant, Constable Kunzig here," Brian said. "Constable Drake and I are on the ferry to Tsawwassen as requested by Staff Sergeant Jenkins. I have the license number, VIN number and a Hertz rental ID number for the subject vehicle, and Constable Drake has a significant number of pictures of the vehicle and its occupants on the digital camera."

After writing down the information, the staff sergeant told the two to just stay on board, out of sight of the present load of passengers and then make the return trip to Nanaimo. Once the ferry left Tsawwassen terminal for the trip back, they were to contact the captain and see if they could download the contents of the camera to one of the ship's computers, then send them to him by E-mail. Having passed on these instructions, Staff Sergeant Blake quickly dialed the number for Hertz Reservations in Vancouver, and after a brief wait, found out that the vehicle in question had been rented Friday morning at the Vancouver Airport location and was scheduled for return before 6:00 p.m. that evening.

Corporal Kent picked up the phone in the detachment office at Vancouver International Airport on the seventh ring. He had just finished making a fresh pot of coffee in anticipation of the shift change and had to finish pouring the water and quickly put the pot in place before dashing for the phone. He then hastily wrote down some very precise instructions given by a staff sergeant at the Island District Criminal Investigation Section and rushed into the watch commander's office.

"Sergeant," Kent said, "we have just been instructed to intercept a returning Hertz rental supposedly arriving anytime now, a gray Ford Explorer, and once the occupants are out of sight, move it to a location where a lab team can do a thorough inside and out analysis of the entire vehicle. We are also to put a very discrete surveillance team on the occupants of the vehicle and maintain it until we determine their final destination. They are potential suspects or witnesses in a homicide investigation that is being kept very quiet. We're going to have to call in extra help for this one."

Mr. Charles Woodrow carefully reviewed the computer generated Hertz bill, then paid in cash and left the counter with his associate, Mr. Brock Adams. Without realizing that they had been photographed once again, they took their time as they strolled through the airport to the WestJet gate for the 6:30 p.m. Calgary flight. They then sat down with their newly purchased magazines and waited for the flight to be called. As soon as they had disappeared from view at the Hertz counter, a plainclothes RCMP constable began going over the paperwork from their rental; confirming the driver's name, operator's license description and the Calgary address given on the rental agreement and indicated on the license. After making copies, he went back to his office computer and located the airline reservation for Mr. Woodrow's flight to Calgary. He then ran the driver's license information and quickly determined that there was no Alberta motor vehicle record of the driver, or that particular Calgary address. He reported this to the sergeant, who told the surveillance team by radio to be even more alert and cautious about being spotted. The team continued to observe the individuals until they boarded their flight and watched as the aircraft took off.

The majority of the arriving Vancouver passengers from the WestJet flight to Calgary quickly made their way towards the baggage claim area, happily greeting the family members who had met them. Two arriving businessmen, seemingly traveling together, followed a slightly different routine that involved heading for the nearest bar. After an hour of conversation replete with drinks and snacks, the two headed for the Air Canada gate for the 9:00 p.m. flight to Vancouver. This was noted by an RCMP surveillance team who had attempted to confirm their reservations for the flight. The names that they entered into the computer did not appear on the passenger list. The gate agent's telephone rang shortly after that and the agent was quietly requested to note the names of two businessmen as they boarded the aircraft. The quiet ones currently seated in the last row of the gate area. She did that and after the flight took off, Calgary Airport Detachment notified Vancouver Airport Detachment that Mr. Dominic Salvatore and Mr. John Sabatini could be expected on the next arriving flight from Calgary. There should be no trouble identifying them, since they looked remarkably like Mr. Charles Woodrow and Mr. Brock Adams whom they had been observing earlier that evening.

The two individuals of interest went their separate ways the moment they got off the plane, both scuttling off to widely separated areas of the short-term parking lot. Fortunately, the delays entailed in lining up to pay the parking fee provided just enough time for the unmarked RCMP cruisers to be in place to begin the tail. Equally fortunate, processing the data that was obtained from the airline in Calgary had yielded drivers license numbers and confirmed addresses in Vancouver. Mr. Sabatini chose to drive directly to his East Fifty-second Avenue home. Mr. Salvatore, despite the late hour, went to his office in the Quality Hotel and Restaurant Supply Co. warehouse on Commercial Drive where all the lights in this large complex were still blazing.

Sixteen

As the Hanley car rolled off the 3:30 p.m. ferry from Campbell River, Mike had to put his finger to his lips and gently shake his head "No" as Constable Ed Brewer started over to greet them. He continued out of the terminal area and on down to Quathiaski Cove Road where he pulled into the Whiskey Point Resort parking lot. After registering and checking into their room with its great view of the ferry terminal and the cove beyond, he left Susan to fend for herself while he strolled up to the detachment office on West Road, trying to look like a big city tourist as he went. When he opened the door, however, the people inside immediately got to their feet to welcome him, even if he wasn't in uniform, since casually dressed commissioned officers don't normally visit small detachments on Saturday afternoons. After being introduced by Corporal Mullet to all the people from the Campbell River Detachment that he didn't know, he asked everyone to sit down and give him an update on the status of the investigation.

Ken Mullet then reported that the crime lab people had finished examining Constable Novak's patrol vehicle in the driveway where it had been parked and determined that no one had touched it but Johnny. They all agreed that it could now be returned to service. Six two-person crews were going through dumpsters, but had not found anything of interest yet. The lab team was now concentrating on the beach area and was starting to exhume and examine the body. Ken suggested to Inspector Hanley that they go to the scene now since it would be getting dark soon. As they got up to leave, Mike heard the phone ring in the living quarters through the hallway door and seconds later Marge Mullet came in to tell Ken that Susan Hanley had invited she and Doreen Brewer out for dinner, since she figured that the rest of the detachment crew had more to think about than eating. That reminded Mike to have the word passed to the team that they would all get together for pizza and a follow-up discussion at 8:00 p.m. He then gave the detachment clerk three twenty-dollar bills and asked her to order the pizza.

Mike, with Corporal Mullet driving the patrol cruiser, rapidly saw how deserted the crime area was as they left the built up area of the island. When they arrived at the scene they saw that the Sam's Wholesale Hardware truck had backed into the lane leading to the beach, effectively blocking any view of their activities from the road. Ken once again backed his unit into the driveway where Johnny had parked the night before, not only to get off the road but also to show the inspector why it had been so hard to find the vehicle this morning. They then walked to the lane, down past the mobile lab unit and onto the beach. Two lab people and the coroner were carefully examining the body and the gravesite in the sand, while four more were on the beach closer to the lane passing scoops of sand through strainers trying to find bullets, skull fragments or anything else of interest.

The sergeant in charge of the team came over to give Mike a progress report. In photographing the scene when they first arrived it was obvious, as Ken had reported earlier that the beach area had been raked smooth to cover whatever activity had gone on during the night. It was fortunate that the calm sunny day had precluded the sand surface from returning to its natural wind blown contours before they had arrived. At the afternoon low tide there had been signs in the gravel and stones below the high water mark that the keel of a small boat had been dragged partially onto the beach, but the waves of the incoming tide had probably rearranged them again by now. Plaster casts had been taken of the tire tracks in the lane before the lab was backed in. The bullet entering Johnny's head had done massive damage, indicating a large caliber weapon at almost point blank range. He must have been taken completely by surprise by whomever was behind him in the dark.

The examination of the body at the gravesite was completed and the mournful task of bagging it and carrying it into the lab vehicle began. Ken couldn't watch, he just turned and looked out over the bay until the crew had finished, saying several prayers as he did so. Mike came up beside him and put his hand on his shoulder.

"You can't blame yourself," Mike said, "training and supervision can only do so much. The best of both was provided, but the individual still has the responsibility to apply the training received.

The real job now is to concentrate on finding the people responsible and putting them away."

"Quadra 2, Quadra 1."

"Quadra 1, Quadra 2," Ken responded into his portable radio.

"Dumpster bonanza, details when we see you."

"Quadra 1, 10-4."

The lab team sergeant calculated that they had another hour before it was completely dark, bringing about the need to start the portable generator and rig the floodlights. Every one on the team now concentrated on the sand-sifting job in the most likely areas. The first positive result was finding the spent cartridge, which closely determined the location of the actual shooting with respect to the burial site and the end of the lane. This was carefully marked, measured and photographed. Half-an-hour later, having used an approximate distance radius from the cartridge location for guidance, a large caliber bullet was sifted out and shortly after, skull fragments. Nothing else unusual was uncovered by dark, so it was agreed that the lab team had completed its job on the beach. The real investigative work now had to begin.

Sam's Wholesale Hardware truck rolled into the ferry terminal and parked in a holding lane out of the way of boarding traffic, since it would wait for the 10:00 p.m. sailing. It had taken a detour on the way to the terminal into the area behind the school where the dumpsters were located, where two plastic garbage bags had been loaded. The driver carefully locked all the doors and then strolled up to West Road and into the detachment building. The kitchen in the living quarters had been transformed into a combination conference room and pizza parlor. Someone had found a case of beer for the now off-duty crew with plenty of cola for the rest. With people sitting wherever they could find a spot, including the floor and with pizza in hand the summary began.

Mike started by discussing everything that they now knew, asking the others to correct or supplement his summarization as he went along. He also asked that someone record the discussions. The evidence so far indicated that:

Constable John Novak in the course of his routine night patrol, or because something had aroused his suspicions, had come upon an illegal activity of sufficient magnitude that the perpetrators had no compulsion about the cold blooded killing of a member of the force. Constable Novak had not followed proper procedures by advising the communications center of his location or requesting backup before approaching the scene.

- The illegal activity took place on a deserted beach, after dark, indicating that some form of smuggling was the likely activity. Evidence indicated that a motor vehicle was present, tire tracks had been recorded, and there was an indication that a boat had been on the beach. By implication, some sort of vessel located just offshore must have been part of the operation. The perpetrators had gone to considerable trouble to conceal all signs of beach activity.

A spent cartridge, bullet and human skull fragments, most probably from the victim, had been located at the scene. A large caliber handgun with silencer had been found concealed in a trash bag in a dumpster located between the crime scene and the ferry terminal. The trash bag also contained sand covered rubber boots and coveralls. A second bag containing rubber boots and coveralls was also discovered as was a rake. The rake had been taken back to the scene and photographic evidence obtained indicating that the distance between the tines exactly matched the raked pattern in the beach sand.

A suspicious vehicle had visited the island overnight on Friday. It was suspicious only because the size of the vehicle and the attire of the occupants did not fit the normal pattern of late Friday evening/early Saturday morning traffic at this time of year. Nothing so far positively located it at the crime scene. Due to some quick thinking and follow up by retired Staff Sergeant Gus Jenkins who had seen the car on the ferry while proceeding to Campbell River, Nanaimo detectives had identified it as a rental unit and photographs of the vehicle and occupants had been taken. A laboratory team analysis of the car was underway now at the Vancouver Airport location where the car had been rented.

At this point of the festivities Mike declared a fifteen-minute break and while the others lined up for the bathroom, he went to the detachment office to use the phone. After briefing the superintendent at home, he called his own office at Island District to tell Staff Sergeant Blake what was going on. John Blake had news of his own to pass on, particularly that the rental car occupants had been identified through car rental and airline sources. They had used phony names and forged drivers' licenses for the car rental and some air travel, and then used their real names for a flight back to Vancouver from Calgary. "E" Division personnel were busy conducting follow-up background checks. The photographs taken of them on the Tsawwassen Ferry and at the airport were available to Mike and the Quadra Island crew on the computer. Mike thanked John for coordinating things at the office and told him to head home until Monday, since they were now dependent on the continuing efforts of the lab teams to make additional progress, with emphasis being placed on matching the sand samples taken from the beach, the deck of the ferries and the automobile tire treads. This would at least verify that the rental car was actually at the scene even if there was no positive proof that the occupants had been.

Mike reconvened the meeting and told them of the developments in the "off-island" part of the investigation. He asked Ken to print out the photographs of the suspect automobile and its occupants for them all to look at, and also to have Gus confidentially show them to the other ferry personnel to confirm their presence on the island.

Even though no evidence specifically placed them at the crime scene so far, it would at least confirm their presence in the vicinity. Mike adjourned the formal part of the gathering at this point and suggested that when the pizza and beer were all gone that everyone head home for a well-deserved rest. He asked the mobile crime lab team to have the vehicle repainted with its normal markings first thing on Monday morning. He also told Ken that the constables on loan from Campbell River would handle the 911 calls for the balance of the weekend shifts so that he and Ed Brewer could get some rest.

SEVENTEEN

Corporal Ken Mullet was incredibly tired as he climbed the stairs to the master bedroom. After seeing all the visitors out and making sure that the relief night constable was familiar with the Saturday night patrol routine on the island, he was really dragging. It had been the longest, shittiest, day of his life. After he had completed his bathroom routine and climbed into bed beside Marge, who seemed to be asleep, he was ready to turn out the light. At this point Marge came alive, enveloped him with her nude body, her nipples already erect in anticipation. She grabbed him by an intimate part of his anatomy, stroked him to full erection and said that it was time for some serious morale boosting in this detachment. In between kisses, she whispered that according to the plan invented by Susan during dinner, Doreen and Ed Brewer as well as Inspector and Mrs. Hanley would be engaged in similar exercises at this time, but they were not to compare notes in the morning.

Sunday morning was windy and raining in the normal late October pattern, in contrast with the day before with its cool breeze and bright sunshine. The Mullet's, Brewer's and Hanley's were gathered for a casual breakfast in the detachment residence kitchen when Gus Jenkins and his wife arrived to join them. Gus had shown the pictures taken yesterday to Steve Mercer and other ferry personnel on both shifts. They had positively identified the car and the businessmen as the ones who had been onboard. Everyone concluded that there was very little more investigation that could be done on the island just now, but Gus reiterated that the normal routine must be continued with no mention of the incident to the local population if they ever hoped to solve the case.

Gus felt very strongly that whatever had gone down would be repeated, since he was sure that Johnny had stumbled onto an activity in progress that may have been part of a pattern of activities that had been going on for a long time. In the middle of the tourist season, the comings and goings of Ford Explorer wouldn't be noticed but at this time of year it would. He explained that the best approach on the island now would be to observe every suspicious non-residential automobile very carefully with the ferry captains and mates being a part of the confidential plan to alert the detachment of similar vehicles arriving in the same time frame. Gus thought that if things were kept quiet with no mention of the disappearance of a member of the force, the perpetrators would repeat their activity, especially if either immigrant or drug smuggling had been involved.

On Monday morning, Ken called Inspector Lee and asked for an immediate replacement for Johnny. He also began to pass the word around the community that Constable Novak had been transferred to a much larger detachment to enhance his training and that a replacement would arrive shortly. Since Johnny had not been on the island very long, nobody paid much attention, although a certain waitress at the terminal coffee shop thought that it was strange that he hadn't stopped in for a farewell cup of coffee.

Eighteen

It was an extremely cold November morning with wind gusts and heavy snow flurries making conditions much worse than usual as the coffin was carried down the front steps of the small church in Humboldt, Saskatchewan after the Mass of the Resurrection. Members of Johnny's graduation troop from "Depot" Division were pallbearers, with two other troops and members of the force from throughout the Province in attendance. The Commanding Officer of "F" division, the Officer Commanding Island District, and Corporal and Mrs. Ken Mullet escorted Johnny's grieving parents. After interment in the mausoleum, the people gathered in the Novak home and quietly discussed the tragedy of a stray hunter's bullet ending the life of such a promising young man. Ken Mullet privately renewed his vow to see that whoever was responsible for this was captured, the real story revealed to his parents, and Johnny's name added to the Roll of Honor of the Force.

Part II

The Distributors

Nineteen

Every morning at 5:30 a.m. the large refrigerated delivery trucks with the QHRS logo moved out of their individual loading docks and began to leave the Quality Hotel and Restaurant Supply Company warehouse complex in a nose to tail line-up similar to circus elephants on parade. They made their way out onto Commercial Drive, on the east side of Vancouver, and then spread out to begin their daily delivery rounds throughout Greater Vancouver, New Westminster and the Fraser Valley. Some make the longer trip by ferry to the urban areas of Vancouver Island, to the Sechelt Peninsula, or up Highway 99 to the Whistler Mountain ski resorts. They each contained a selection of the finest quality meats, fish, fruit, vegetables, bakery and dairy products so essential to the successful operation of first class hotels and restaurants. In the summer season, they provide for the needs of the cruise ships sailing to Alaska in addition to the long term provisioning contracts to supply the large variety of commercial ships trading in and out of Vancouver area ports. All of this was due to the vision of the company founders. In 1896, Giuseppi Salvatore merged his wholesale produce company with Antonio Battista's butcher shop and they began to offer free delivery to their best customers in the neighborhood.

The warehouse complex includes a large well-lit display area where executive chefs and restaurant owners can gather at any hour to inspect the freshness and quality of the products offered, place their orders, and enjoy the hospitality of the customer lounge where excellent wines and appropriate snacks are always available. But most of the regular customers only visit occasionally, preferring to place their order sheets with the delivery drivers each day. One side of the main warehouse has rows of unloading docks where incoming deliveries are received from the tractor-trailer rigs, and the opposite side has the rows of loading docks where the company trucks back in each evening, plug in their refrigeration units, and are cleaned and made ready for loading the next day's orders. In between are the massive storerooms and refrigerated chambers, climate controlled to just the right temperature to preserve the freshness of the contents of the rooms.

Attached to one end of the warehouse is the three-story building containing the executive offices and the sales, purchasing and accounting departments. The ground floor has a large employee lunchroom, a drivers' lounge and a general office area. This office contains the long counters where the drivers turn in their daily delivery receipt forms at one end and their regular customer order sheets at the other. The order sheets are reviewed, data entered into the computer, itemized prices totaled and then sent on to the loading foreman's office in the warehouse where the crews are responsible for having each truck loaded and ready to go by the morning departure time.

In recent years, a large separate annex was added which included a room near the front where drivers could go to hand in their daily special order cash receipts and place their special orders for the next business day. These orders are then packaged and prepared for loading by a dedicated group working in the secure part of the complex. A separate accounting department handled the data for this newest segment of the business.

The company is still privately held by members of the Salvatore and Battista founding families with the fourth generation just moving up to take over the reins of management. The profit levels continue to grow, although the winter business, when so much has to be imported from warmer climates, is not as lucrative as the booming summer activities. It was to supplement the slower winter season that an enterprising young family member suggested the addition of the special orders department. Because of the investments made by other branches of the family in a South American shipping company, import/export firms and large farms and orchards throughout Canada and the United States, extremely reliable and cost effective sources of supply are ensured. Quality is tightly controlled, since everyone is aware of increasing competition and the need to maintain a large customer base for continuing growth.

Twenty

Chuck Rossi eased the big truck around the corner from Burrard Street onto the street behind the stately old hotel in downtown Vancouver and slowly moved down to the kitchen loading area. One advantage of starting out so damn early every morning was that the downtown traffic was still light, and he could make his center city deliveries on time before moving further out on his route to the places south along Granville and west on Broadway. As soon as the truck pulled to a stop, his helper jumped out, opened the side door of the truck, and pulled the loading ramp out to the edge of the loading dock. By then, Chuck had entered the rear door of the kitchen supply area and shouted out a greeting to the staff. After making sure that they were ready to receive the order, Chuck motioned for the helper to start bringing in the frozen goods.

After seeing the unloading process started, he went back to the truck and opened the driver's side door. Reaching for the latch release he pulled the seat back down onto the seat, revealing a two-foot high door with a combination lock built into the structure behind the cab. Looking around and seeing no one, he moved the lock dial the prescribed number of turns each way and swung the door open, revealing a steel cupboard with shelves holding neat rows of partially filled plastic bags of the kind the supermarkets use for groceries. He carefully removed five of the bags, sat them on the cab floor, closed and locked the door, then moved the seat back up to its normal position.

Gathering up the bags, he went back into the hotel and proceeded down the hall to the bell captain's desk in the lobby. He met one of the bellhops who was waiting and quietly passed one of the bags to him. In exchange, he received cash and a note requesting a delivery for the next day. He then went to the housekeeper's office, the shoeshine stand, the coffee shop and the gift shop where similar transactions took place. Going back down the hall, through the loading area and out to the truck, he repeated the process of opening the safe door. He then put the cash and order forms into an empty bag and locked things up again.

Meanwhile, in the kitchen receiving area, Executive Chef John Cassidy, was meticulously checking off each item on his copy of the order form as Chuck's helper continued to bring the boxes in. John was a big man, tall and muscular, who had first learned his profession as a cook in the navy. It had not been his first choice of occupational trades when he joined, but he was good at it and he soon came to enjoy the work, particularly as he received compliments from the crew on his cooking and baking skills. A good cook is essential to good morale, and John progressively became one of the best. After retiring from the navy as a Chief Petty Officer, he joined the staff of the hotel's restaurant as a line cook and gradually made his up through the ranks as his abilities became known. He had been instrumental in vastly increasing the amount of banquet and convention business in the hotel due to the quality of the products produced by his kitchens and thus was a very important customer of the Quality Hotel and Restaurant Supply Company.

When Chuck came over to him as the last boxes of fresh citrus fruit were brought in, John completed and signed the driver's form acknowledging receipt of all the items ordered. He then asked Chuck if he had a minute to spare to discuss something personal.

"I really need a favor from your management Chuck, and I would appreciate it if you could help me. My wife's sister died recently up in northern Alberta and left her only child an orphan. He is just seventeen with one term left to complete his high school education, so Anne and I have agreed to take him in since the other sister in Alberta can't afford to keep him on the farm. I know that he is trying to put some money together for college and needs a part time job, so I would like you to ask your boss if he could possibly do something for me."

"I don't know, Mr. Cassidy. The company normally hires only family members or people closely connected with and recommended by the families. I don't think there is much chance of him getting on with us." "Well," replied John after a long pause, "I think that I've been a pretty steady customer over the years. I'm not asking for anything other than giving a hard working young man a chance in life. Just you go and ask your senior management about it and let me know what they have to say when you come back tomorrow."

Chuck promised to see what he could do, then went out to the truck where the helper was securing the side door. *Shit, he thought, just what I don't need, something to screw up one of the best accounts on the route.* With that, he put the truck in gear and moved on to the hotel on Georgia Street, which was next on the delivery route.

When the trucks return to the warehouse in the afternoon, the helpers go to the employee lunchroom for a hot meal before going home. The drivers first go to the general office to complete the daily paperwork, then to the special order department to turn in the cash receipts and place the orders for the next day. They are then free to go to the drivers' lounge for a late lunch and a glass of wine. Due to extenuating circumstances, Chuck varied his normal afternoon routine and first went up to the third floor executive suite where he asked to see Mr. Salvatore.

After being ushered into his uncle's office, he explained the unusual request that he had received from his best customer. Motioning for him to sit down, Dom Salvatore called his partners to discuss the situation and the final consensus was that they give the kid a part time job and carefully watch just where they used him and with whom he worked. Chuck was relieved at the decision, but was also pissed at being seriously chewed out by Dom for a problem that he didn't create. He was, after all, just the messenger. The good news though, was the opportunity to show his customer that he did have some influence with management and had the ability to deliver when favors were needed.

Twenty-one

The clouds totally obscured the mountains on the North Shore and the cold winter rain fell continuously as the Greyhound bus turned off of Main Street and into the bus and railway terminal. At 7:30 a.m. on a cold December 27, the crowd getting off the bus on the first working day after the holidays didn't look very cheerful. The bus had very few people on board during the all night trip through the Rocky Mountains from Edmonton, but many commuters had boarded as the route continued through the Fraser Valley suburbs and into Vancouver.

One of the last passengers to leave the bus was a tall, gangly young man who looked about seventeen. He was wearing a backpack and was carrying a well-worn suitcase held together by a frayed leather belt. He looked around with some degree of confusion, then spotted the entrance to the main terminal where he headed directly for the men's room and was relieved of some of the discomfort of continuous day and night bus travel. Grooming himself as best he could, he then went out and found the bank of payphones and rummaged through the backpack until he located a carefully folded sheet of paper. Dropping in his coins, he dialed the number.

"Hello," responded a pleasant female voice on the telephone.

"Hello, Aunt Anne, it's Billy. Bill Patterson. I've just arrived

98

in Vancouver and I need directions to your house."

"Oh, Billy, I'm so relieved to hear from you. Your uncle said that you would probably get into town soon and I've been waiting for your call. Now, this is what you do to get here."

Carefully following the directions, Bill walked across Main Street to the Skytrain Station and boarded an eastbound train to Broadway. He then went over to Commercial Drive and waited for the Number Twenty Victoria trolley bus, which he climbed on and traveled to Fifty-eight Avenue. After carefully crossing the heavily traveled Victoria Drive and walking two blocks to the east he opened the gate, walked up the front steps, and rang the doorbell. He was finally home.

Sipping his tea and enjoying the fresh scones with strawberry jam that his aunt had placed in front of him as soon as he got his coat off, he truly felt welcome. For the first time since leaving home after his mother's death he was somewhat settled. Just being in a normal home environment again after so long, made a big difference in comfort level. The advanced planning that his aunt had done for him made him feel more relaxed and much less nervous about his situation.

"Today," Anne said, "you get caught up with your rest. Your uncle won't be home until after three this afternoon, so you'll have time to nap before dinner. Tomorrow morning we have an appointment with the high school principal at 10:00 a.m., so that we can get you registered for school. I also understand that your uncle plans to take you to the Quality Hotel and Restaurant Supply Company warehouse in the afternoon so that you can see about a part time job. Lots to do before the New Year's holiday begins."

When Bill had finished all of the scones that he could reasonably get away with, Anne showed him to his room in the finished part of the basement. The bedroom was near the foot of the basement stairs just off the hallway leading to the outside entrance to the backyard. The wood paneled room was small with two windows, one facing the street and the other the side yard. There was a small adjoining bathroom with shower, and in Bill's experience, it was the most luxurious setup he had ever seen. He put his gear down and gave his aunt a grateful hug, saying that he would take a nap and then see what he could do to make himself useful around the place. Anne told him not to worry about that, just to relax and come upstairs whenever he was rested. Then she went out, quietly closing the door behind her. Bill took his time unpacking and putting his things away as neatly as he could. Most of his clothes were wrinkled after their long stay in the suitcase, so he would have to do some washing and ironing in the next day or two. He sat down on the bed and pulled of his boots for the first time in almost forty-eight hours, then lay back with a sigh. Before dozing off, he once again relived the extraordinary events that had occurred in his life during the past year.

Twenty-two

The sudden November afternoon death of Bill Patterson's father in the fields behind the family farmhouse near Fairview, Alberta had come as a terrible shock to both he and his mother. The instant change from the hard but happy life they were experiencing on the farm in Peace River country to dealing with the tragedy which had so suddenly taken place had been overwhelming. His mother had been bustling around in the kitchen putting the final touches on dinner while he did his homework. The realization suddenly came to both of them that his father hadn't come in from the fields as soon as darkness approached. This was so unusual that Billy immediately put on his parka and headed out the door to check the barn to see if the tractor was back. His dad had gone out after lunch to check the perimeter fences and do whatever repairs were necessary before the onset of the heavy winter snows. Normally, he would have been back in shortly after Billy had walked up the driveway after getting off the Fairview High School bus, but there was no sign of him as the full moon began to rise in the darkening night sky.

Billy shouted out several times as he walked around the barn and the old stable in the yard, but there was only silence in return, not even a hint of the sound of a tractor engine in the distance. He went back into the house to get the keys to the pickup truck so that he could drive out and look for his dad. Meanwhile, his mother called her sister, Elsie, at the next farm down the road to ask if her husband, Hank, had seen Jim out in the fields. The answer came back, "No," but Hank and their son would immediately get into their truck and go out looking also. Nancy Patterson had such a terrible feeling of foreboding that she called the police emergency number, even though she had nothing real to base her fears on.

Constable Cy Perkins responded to the radio dispatch and immediately drove to the detachment office. He parked the patrol car, got into the four by four with the twin spotlights on the roof, and headed out towards the Patterson farm. He saw the two pickup trucks off in the distance driving the perimeter, so he turned out into the fields on a direct path from the barn towards the back boundaries of the farm. He had only gone a half-mile when he saw the tractor, engine running, and the person lying on the ground beside it. He jumped out, checked Jim over and saw at once that it was too late. Hand clutching his chest and face contorted in death from the pain of the heart attack, absolutely nothing could be done. Cy returned to the four by four and called for the coroner, the NCOIC of the Detachment and Father Murphy, the parish priest. He then shut off the tractor and waited beside the body to keep predators away until help could arrive.

After the funeral, Billy had offered to quit school and work full time to keep the farm operating, but his mother would not hear of it. His education was too important, particularly since he was in his senior year with only one semester remaining until graduation, and plans made to go on to Fairview College. So his mother had agreed with her sister's suggestion that the two farms be worked in common, Hank running things with the two boys helping out part time through the winter and a full time farm hand to be hired in the spring.

The next blow came when Billy returned home from school on a snowy February afternoon to find his mother on the couch, doubled up in pain. He immediately called his Aunt Elsie, then got his mother into the truck and headed for Fairview Hospital. After waiting for what seemed like hours, his aunt and the doctor came to tell him that his mother would have to be admitted for several days of testing. He then began the routine of driving the truck to school each day so that he could visit the hospital after classes.

Billy's mother rapidly grew worse, the diagnosis was pancreatic cancer, which had spread throughout the abdomen and was not considered treatable. The staff went out of their way to keep her comfortable and to be there for Billy. Mercifully, for everyone concerned, the end came quickly. Bill Patterson was an orphan.

The occurrence of his mother's death so soon after losing his father was devastating, even with the small family and long time friends gathering around to console him and provide as much support as they could. His Aunt Anne and her husband, John Cassidy, came from Vancouver for the funeral and stayed with him in the house for a few days. Her sister, his Aunt Elsie, wanted him to move in with her and Hank, but he preferred to stay in the house alone and just visit periodically for meals. Constable Perkins dropped by to say, "Hello," whenever his routine patrols took him near the Patterson farm. To suppress his grief and loneliness, Billy really dug into his schoolwork and increased his activities with the local Army Cadet unit that he had belonged to all throughout high school. Thinking ahead to graduation in June, he began to have serious thoughts about a military career.

During his periodic trips to town on weekends to buy supplies, he got into the habit of going by the RCMP detachment office just to chat with Constable Perkins or Corporal George for a little while before going home. Often, Mrs. George would invite him to stay on for dinner. Eventually, when he brought up the subject of a military career, they offered an alternative, and explained all of the requirements necessary to become an RCMP cadet. With some degree of excitement Billy recognized that he already met most of the entry requirements and now had an immediate goal for life after high school graduation.

The following Monday, Billy went directly to the detachment office after school and asked Corporal George to go over the requirements with him once more. Corporal George was initially concerned about Bill's age, since a cadet had to be at least nineteen at the time of entry and Bill appeared to be no more than seventeen. Billy assured him that there was no problem since he turned nineteen a week after high school graduation. He was glad that he looked younger than his age, especially since he was really the oldest one in his high school class after being held back for an additional year in kindergarten at St. Thomas More School at the recommendation of Sister Margaret. It had all turned out for the best since he'd been at or near the top of his class for the rest of his school career.

The other requirements were not a concern; he had a driver's license and a clean record, proficiency on the computer, skinny but strong as an ox from working on the farm all his life, proficient in sports at school, especially track and soccer, and had learned close order drill and the parade ground routine with the army cadets. He was also grateful that he had obtained a St John Ambulance first aid certificate through the cadet corps. Since the only thing he seemed to be missing was a CPR certificate and Fairview College was sponsoring the course again in two weeks, Corporal George arranged for Bill's visit to Edmonton to take the Recruit Selection Test and the physical ability and medical examinations.

Graduation day was bright and sunny at Fairview High School. The graduation ceremonies were well done as usual and the feelings of pride and accomplishment mixed with a slight fear of the future pervaded the graduating class. Bill missed his parents terribly, but Aunt Elsie and Uncle Jim were there for him, as was Aunt Anne who had driven all the way from Vancouver for the week. Just having her in the house cooking and cleaning as his mother had done made the week very special. They were also there for him at the Greyhound Depot as he boarded the bus for Regina to enter Cadet Troop Forty-two at the RCMP Training Academy, "Depot" Division.

✸
Twenty-three

B ill arrived at the academy a day before the June one start
date of his training. He found himself one of twenty-
four members of Troop Forty-two, which was made up
of twelve men and twelve women from all over the country.
Having just turned nineteen, Bill was the youngest in his troop
and possibly the youngest in the division, which was certainly
a change from being the oldest in his class all through high
school. Unlike many others, Bill had little trouble adjusting to
the training routine. He was used to getting up at 5:30 every
morning on the farm. He was also used to the parade ground drill
from his years with the army cadets, he thought the cafeteria
food was wonderful (compared with his own cooking during the
last few weeks) and as usual he excelled at running, leaving the
rest of the troop winded and far behind.

As time went on, however, he found many things that were
not so easy. Other troop members had university degrees, prior
auxiliary police training and a lot of business experience. So he
worked out many trade relationships, exchanging extra coaching
in physical training for assistance with applied police sciences
homework, and parade ground skills for criminal code drills.
Being naturally cheerful, he got along well with everyone,
frustrating the drill instructors who tried to grind him down to

size but couldn't do much to dampen his enthusiasm for what he really enjoyed doing. His physical strength from years of farm work amazed his instructors, because he looked too tall and skinny to be taken as a serious threat to anyone. He was also very good on the firing range, farmyard practice and army cadet camp training had given him good skills with rifle and pistol shooting. But the paperwork exercises often had him bogged down and looking for help.

Halfway through the twenty-four week training program, police defensive tactics were put to good use during the detachment exercises, which provided realistic training at the academy's Buffalo Detachment. Bill could outrun and catch the volunteer wrongdoers but often had trouble subduing and cuffing them since he didn't want to hurt anyone. He soon became more proficient though when he was sometimes forcibly reminded that his real world suspects were not going to be gentle with him. The days began to go by quickly now as graduation approached and the cadets were given the opportunity to express their preferences for initial postings to a detachment for their six months of on-the-job training. No one really expected to receive their selected posting because the needs of the force were probably very different from their own. Bill didn't request any particular posting but he did indicate the type of work he would like to do in the future.

Graduation day arrived at the end of November and Regina's winter had arrived with it. The last four weeks were a blur, alternating between very hard work and impressive events such as the Troop Regimental Dinner. The graduation parade was held outside accompanied by wind and periodic snow showers, probably planned to acquaint them with life in "G" Division in the Northwest Territories, but other ceremonial activities were conducted in the drill hall. Proud family members watched the final dismissal and as the new constables joined their celebrating family members, Bill realized once more just how alone he really was. None of his family members were able to attend, since the icy winter weather had precluded travel from the Peace River Valley and the Cassidy's were not able to get away from Vancouver due to a big weekend function being held at the hotel where Uncle John worked.

After spending some time visiting the family groups of his friends, Bill quietly went back to his room. Unlike everyone else in his troop, he hadn't yet received his detachment posting orders and wasn't able to make any travel plans. He would have to spend the rest of the weekend lounging around in the barracks wondering why he had been told to report to the sergeant major's office first thing on Monday morning.

Bill marched into the sergeant major's office precisely at 08:00 a.m. on Monday morning and stood rigidly at attention, one meter in front of the desk. "Constable Patterson reporting as ordered Sergeant Major."

"At ease, constable. Have a seat and relax. We need to chat a little bit about your first posting. By now you should be wondering why you didn't receive orders like the rest of your troop, but I had to wait until they had all left the division before I could have this discussion with you. The powers that be took note that on your preference form you had expressed an interest in undercover work, but in the normal course of events it would be at least a year in a detachment before you could even volunteer. However, a special case has come up where you might just fill the bill if you really have an interest. I must warn you; however, that it could be extremely dangerous. A young constable has already lost his life in the preliminary stages of this case."

As the sergeant major went into more detail, it became obvious that he was really the only one available that could take on this assignment. An orphan with relatives in Vancouver, young enough to still be in high school and with an uncle having the right business connections to make it all work. He didn't hesitate very long at all before he formally volunteered for the job.

The sergeant major then told him to pack his uniforms for long term storage and be prepared to fly to Montreal that afternoon to enter into a three week undercover training course that might just teach him enough to save his life. As Bill got to his feet to leave, the sergeant major mentioned that the course would end two days before Christmas. He was to return to "Depot" Division on December twenty-third, and spend the holiday with the sergeant major and his wife. On Boxing Day, he would be sent on his way to begin his new life.

Twenty-four

I t was a crisp sunny morning as Bill and his aunt waited at the bus stop on Victoria Drive. There was still frost on the ground in the shade under the trees, but the sun was slowly warming things up to a temperature that was positively tropical compared to a late December day at home, or in Montreal, for that matter. As he recalled the frantic pace of the last few weeks, the Number Twenty Granville bus came along, heading for downtown. They stayed on the bus as far as Broadway then transferred to a Broadway cross-town bus which took them to Penticton Avenue and the venerable Vancouver Technical High School.

As they walked up to the nearest entrance of the school building, Anne stopped in her tracks and looked at Bill, "For heavens sake, stop marching. Slow down and slouch a little bit or this whole thing will be a waste of time. You look as though you're leading a parade."

"Sorry, it's really hard to forget twenty-eight weeks of training in just a couple of weeks. I'll try to remember that I always have to imitate the other kids when school starts."

They entered the building and followed the signs through the halls to the general office. Bill was astounded at the size of the school, which had an enrollment of almost 2000 students very different than Fairview High, which had 350 at the best of times. When they finally reached the office, Anne introduced herself and told the secretary that they had an appointment with the principal. After being shown in and introduced to Mr. Lewis, he invited them to sit down and then closed his office door.

"I would like to welcome you to Vancouver Tech, Bill. Inspector Marshall was here last week and explained this highly confidential situation to me. I can see the great risks involved, so naturally I won't know you after today other than as one of many hundreds of students I pass in the hall everyday. I have your files and your transfer paperwork completed. Your classes have been arranged to give you Friday's off and I have managed to get you into enrichment courses so that hard work and good grades will earn you college credits. The down side will be the amount of work involved in keeping up with the others in your classes. I have also enrolled you in the track program and in physical ed so that you can stay in condition. If there are no more questions, the secretary will give you your schedule and a map of the building. Good luck, and someday if you can come back and tell me what is really going on, I would surely appreciate it."

Bill treated his aunt to lunch on the way home using money from his first paycheck, which he had received just before leaving Regina. Of course that had meant stopping at a bank first so that he could open an account and deposit most of it. This would also allow him to arrange for automatic payroll deposit when he got in touch with his "E" Division contact. He had memorized the number and the code name to use which he was to call periodically from widely separated payphones.

Later that afternoon, John Cassidy took his nephew for his job interview. They turned off of Commercial Drive into the

QHRS compound, threading their way between the delivery trucks returning from their daily rounds. They parked in the customer lot outside of the showroom area and went directly into the customer lounge. John took a few minutes to introduce his nephew to his fellow executive chefs who were there to place orders and then took Bill into the general office area.

They went to the nearest desk where John explained that his nephew was here to fill out a job application. The clerk told him that they were not hiring and didn't process application forms from people outside the company. Just then Chuck Rossi came in from his truck and spotted John and a tall skinny kid at the desk. He rushed over and greeted Mr. Cassidy enthusiastically, met Bill Patterson, then asked the clerk to phone upstairs to Mr. Salvatore's office and ask if they could see him. Chuck was given the message to take Mr. Cassidy and his relative to see John Sabatini, the warehouse superintendent.

Getting off the elevator on the third floor, they went down the hall to an office where a large, rumpled man was on the phone chewing someone's ass out for not getting a delivery in on time. He gestured for them to come in and then slammed down the phone.

"Goddamned suppliers think they can deliver their crap any time they feel like it. What the fuck do you want?"

John Cassidy grimaced and Chuck rushed to explain who the visitors were and what they wanted. Sabatini lumbered to his feet and shook hands all round and then said that of course they had a job for the nephew of a good customer. Just go on down, see the warehouse foreman and arrange a starting date. He would call ahead to tell him that they were coming.

So they got back on the elevator and went to the first floor, through the offices, and out to the warehouse where they dodged pallet trucks on they're way into the large dispatch office in the center of the distribution area. Computer operators printed out loading orders and handed them over the counter to the crew chiefs, who promptly had their loading crews move up and down the aisles with their pallet trucks to pick up the boxes to load onto the trucks. Pacing up and down in the middle of the room like a coach on the sidelines of a playoff game was Joe DeSilva, loading foreman, who was overseeing the beginning of the busiest time of the day. The day shift had completed the work of unloading the tractor trailers which brought in the food products from all over the country and the evening crews were now gearing up to load the company trucks for tomorrow mornings deliveries.

Joe gestured at John and Bill to come in and sit down at an empty desk and then brought over an employment form. "Fill this out completely, sign it, and have the signature witnessed," Joe said. "Everything you put down will be checked out. If everything isn't correct when we verify it, you will be fired before you start."

Bill completed the form and pushed it towards his uncle, who read it carefully then witnessed the signature. He looked hard at Bill, obviously hoping that the background work by "E" Division had been thorough. Bill smiled his reassurance, although he had no idea if it would pass company scrutiny or not. It had better, if this assignment was as dangerous as the sergeant major had implied, so things had to be done perfectly. But it really was puzzling since there was nothing obviously dangerous about working in a food warehouse.

Joe came back from yelling at a crew chief, looked over the form, and told Bill that he would work Thursday and Friday evenings from 3:00 to 11:00 p.m., with a thirty- minute break for dinner and two fifteen- minute coffee breaks per shift in the employee lunchroom. No one was permitted to leave the warehouse until the end of the shift. Bill was to go to the company store next to the lunchroom and buy two pair of tan work pants. The company would provide two green work shirts with the company logo. Clean clothes every day, no exception. Warehouse workers wear green, truck drivers wear blue, drivers' helpers wear gray, go get the correct goddamn shirts and see you next Thursday right on time.

Bill was surprisingly nervous as he got off the bus in front of the school on Wednesday morning, and he caught himself marching again as he approached the entrance. He had enjoyed a pleasant New Year's Day yesterday, watching the Rose Bowl Parade on TV with his aunt and uncle, then going out with them for a drive around Stanley Park and a nice dinner at a waterfront restaurant. This had been a treat for John who had worked very late New Year's Eve making sure that everything was perfect for the gala New Year's Eve Dinner Dance at the hotel. But this morning was different for Bill, a very nerve wracking experience. It was bad enough coming into a large, unfamiliar school as an absolute stranger, but it was a whole lot worse coming in as a new undercover constable who didn't know much about basic police work other than training class experience.

There were hundreds of kids in the school hallway as Bill made his way to the office, trying to get through the crowds. He entered, told one of the counselors who he was, was escorted to his assigned locker first and then his homeroom on the second floor. After being introduced to his teacher and given a seat near the front, he was introduced to the rest of the class after the first bell had rung. Naturally, being a new student in a senior class that had been together for years, everyone looked at him curiously and then turned their heads away and totally ignored him. The bell finished ringing at the end of the homeroom session and he was in the classroom doorway studying his school map trying to figure out the best way to his next class. Fortunately, a girl with long auburn hair wearing a neat tartan skirt with a green sweater stopped beside him and quietly asked if she could help.

"Yes, thank you," Bill said. "This school is much bigger than my last one and it's pretty confusing for a newcomer. I'm supposed to be on my way to Advanced English Lit."

"That's easy, that's my next class too. I'm Allison Stuart, welcome to Vancouver Tech. Just come with me."

"Allison, thank you. I'm Bill Patterson from Fairview, Alberta. I just moved in with my aunt and uncle on East Fifty-eight near Victoria Drive."

"I'm not very far from you then; we live on Sixty-second, so I'll probably be seeing you on the bus in the mornings."

At that point they arrived at the classroom door, Bill introduced himself to the teacher and was told where to sit. Once again he was introduced to the class and once again he was totally ignored, except by Allison who gave him a shy smile then turned back to her book. The rest of the school day was much the same, except that he didn't see Allison again and nobody offered to help him. Twice he arrived at class after the bell and was greeted with annoyance by the teacher. Much later, as he stood waiting for the Victoria bus after getting off the Broadway cross town, he spotted Allison talking to some girls who were also waiting for the bus, but she didn't seem to notice him.

The bus was very crowded, filled with students in the typical manner with the noisy, rowdy boys in the back, girls chatting and giggling in the middle and a few serious ones near the front trying to do their homework. Bill and Allison were in the latter group. He deliberately went past his bus stop and got off at the Sixty-first street stop where Allison got off.

"Are you still lost?" Allison said when the bus had moved away, "I thought you lived on Fifty-eighth?"

"I do, but I wanted to thank you again. You're the only one who spoke to me in school all day. At lunchtime, even the kids at the same table ignored me. So I really appreciate your help."

They were walking towards Sixty-second all this time, having crossed Victoria after the bus had gone, but when they reached the intersection Allison stopped. "Thanks for the escort Bill, but you had better turn around now. I don't want my parents to see me walking home with you or I'll have all kinds of explaining to do. If I see you in the cafeteria tomorrow I'll come over and say hello."

"That would be great, because I won't be on the bus tomorrow or Friday afternoon, I have to go to work right after school."

With that, Allison turned and started down Sixty-second while Bill walked back towards Fifty-eighth, convinced now that school wouldn't be so bad after all.

Twenty-five

I t was cloudy and dark with gusty winds and showers blowing across Commercial Drive as Bill got off the bus in front of the QHRS complex at 2:45 p.m. He had practically run out of school to catch the Crosstown and get to Victoria Drive in time to catch a Granville bus for work. He went into the warehouse through the employee's entrance and found the men's locker room next to the lunchroom. He put his name on an empty locker near the back of the room and then got his uniform out of his backpack before putting it away in the locker. He changed quickly and was on the floor by the foreman's office just before 3:00 p.m.

Joe DeSilva greeted him impatiently, called out to a crew chief and asked him to come and get his new helper. Sal Battista came over and introduced himself to Bill, then introduced him to the rest of the crew "We'll get to know each other better during the break," Sal said. "In the meantime we've got trucks to load. We are responsible for trucks fifteen through twenty-eight and we also have to help unload the bakery delivery trucks when they roll in at 9 o'clock. You work with Jerry here and just do everything he tells you to do. You'll catch onto the routine in a few days."

Bill worked very hard for the next four hours and was ready

for the dinner break. He tried to do a little more than the others on the team to show that he could really help and also because lifting all the heavy boxes would help to keep him in shape. As he worked, he also tried to watch what was going on around him, both to learn the routine and to see if there was anything else of interest. By the time 7:00 p.m. rolled around they had loaded truck twenty, and were just over half finished. During the dinner break the team sat together and Sal explained more about the operation. He described how the day shift unloaded the tractor-trailers from the suppliers and put everything away in the storerooms and refrigerators in accordance with the carefully designated stacking locations on the storage charts. Then the sales office made up the specific delivery order forms for each truck, which the loading crews followed when they took the products from storage for loading.

After a few weeks, Bill had learned the job routine very well and was more than pulling his weight as a team member. Sal was pleased with his new helper and said a couple of times that he wished Bill could work every day, but he knew how important getting an education was. Sal had graduated from high school in June two years ago and had been a team leader for eight months. He explained that as the great-great-grandson of one of the founders, he had to work in every department in the entire business for at least six months, then eventually the company would send him to college to learn the skills necessary for management. He didn't know if they wanted him to major in marketing, finance, or just business in general, and he wouldn't know until the time came to go back to school.

A few days later Bill made a men's room visit halfway through the dinner break period and then went to have a look at the loading area when things were quiet. He quickly drew back behind a pillar when he saw a large team of people wearing black shirts come out of the office area carrying large shopping bags. The people spread out and went past the loading doors to each truck, out to the platform, then down to the driver's side door. Bill couldn't see what they were doing but noticed that they came back with the bags empty and folded, and then quickly went back to the office. Bill hurried to his lunchroom table, hoping that no one would comment on where he had been for so long. Fortunately, Jerry was regaling the crew with stories about his latest amorous adventures and nobody paid any attention to Bill as he sat down.

The next day, Bill asked Sal who it was that wore the black uniform shirts, since he had seen a couple of people wearing them near the office door one day. Sal looked at him in surprise then quietly explained that they were part of the large crew who worked in the special orders department and were not normally seen in the warehouse area. He then told Bill that, coincidentally, he was being transferred to special orders within the next two weeks and Jerry would become their new crew chief. Management felt that it was time for Sal to learn something new. Bill indicated that he would really like to become a driver's helper sometime soon, since he had a commercial license from Alberta and would like to learn more about delivery route driving. Sal listened thoughtfully and then mentioned that since Bill had proven himself to be a hard and dedicated worker, he would pass on his request to management.

Bill seemed to be perpetually tired these days. Working two shifts a week in the evenings with four full days at school participating in very difficult courses with all the associated activities and homework, left very little time for recreation. When he saw the posters in school advertising the drama department presentation of the "King and I," he asked Allison during lunch if she would go with him on Tuesday or Wednesday evening next week. They had continued to have lunch together in the cafeteria a couple of times a week and he still walked her part way home from the bus stop after school on the days he didn't work. He had begun to take her hand crossing Victoria Drive and then they naturally continued to hold hands until she said "good-bye" at the corner of Sixty second.

"I don't know, Bill," Allison said. "I would love to go with you and I would love to see the show, but I don't know if my father will let me go with you. I couldn't go out at night by myself, my mother wouldn't mind if I went with you, but my father is a Vancouver City Policeman and is very fussy about who I go out with. He's a detective sergeant and thinks that all teenage boys are punks who constantly get into trouble, so he really won't let me date much at all. But I think he knows your Uncle John, so I'll ask and see what he says. I'll let you know tomorrow."

On the way home from the bus stop that afternoon, Allison reminded Bill that she would ask her parents about the play and let him know tomorrow. Then she said that she really hoped that they could go together, since she considered him to be a really good friend. She gave his hand a final squeeze at Sixty-second then hurried up the street towards home.

Bill was so pleased at the prospect of having a girl friend at last, that he almost forgot to stop at the gas station pay phone on the way home to call his "E" Division contact.

He wanted to pass on the information about the special order crew that he had spotted in the warehouse and mention that he had asked for a better job which would, if he was lucky, offer more visibility into the delivery operations.

At lunch the next day, Allison said that her mother and father had argued about her request to go to the school play. Fortunately, her mother had won out saying that it was about time that Ali had a chance to develop a life of her own before going off to college, since she was already a high school senior. Her father had agreed very reluctantly and said that Bill had to come in to meet him before they left for the school. Bill was pleased and said that he would be happy to meet her parents, but Allison told him to expect some very detailed questions about his background.

When Bill arrived at work that afternoon, he was told by Jerry to go and see Joe DeSilva in the warehouse office. In the midst of the usual controlled pandemonium around the computer terminals and the half-joking obscenities exchanged between crew chiefs at the counter, Joe told Bill that someone in management must like him because word had come down that he was promoted to be a weekend relief driver's helper. He was to go directly to the driver's lounge and ask for Chuck Rossi who would give him the details. Bill went through the general office and knocked on the door of the driver's lounge. When someone opened the door, he asked for Chuck and then waited patiently outside.

"Hello again, Mr. Rossi," Bill said. "Mr. DeSilva told me to come here to see you."

"That's right Bill, Sal Battista recommended you for a helper's job and there have been some retirements and promotions recently. My uncle suggested that you work on the truck with me on Fridays and Saturdays, starting next week. You'll have to be here no later than 5:00 a.m., and you'll be working two-day shifts per week instead of the afternoon shifts. My uncle said that your pay would be the same or perhaps a little more if you continue to work hard and I agreed to it. Make sure that you get the right color shirts and be out at truck fifteen next Friday morning at 5:00 a.m., ready to work."

"Thanks very much, Mr. Rossi, and please tell Sal that I really appreciate his recommendation. Oh, and thank your uncle also. I'll be here Friday morning ready to go."

Precisely at 7:00 p.m. the next Wednesday, Bill walked up the front steps of the Stuart residence and rang the doorbell. The door immediately swung open and a large imposing man in navy blue trousers with broad suspenders pulled over a light blue shirt stood looking at him. He was slightly shorter than Bill but had a very rugged build. "Good evening, sir," Bill said, "I'm Bill Patterson and I'm here to take Allison to the high school play."

Detective Sergeant Stuart just stood there looking Bill up and down then finally gestured for him to come inside and pointed to the living room. He looked very intimidating standing there staring at him in silence, but Bill wasn't particularly intimidated. If someone wanted to wear old police uniform clothing as casual evening wear, it was okay by him. As he entered the room, he saw an attractive woman who was obviously Allison's mother sitting on the couch.

"Good evening Mrs. Stuart, I'm Bill Patterson. I've come to take Allison to the school play."

"How nice to meet you Bill," Margaret Stuart replied. "Allison has been looking forward to going to the performance with you. Sit down, she'll be ready in a minute or two." Bill sat down on the chair opposite the couch as the detective sergeant sat down beside his wife and immediately leaned towards him. "What kind of trouble did you get into in Alberta that prompted you to come all the way to Vancouver to finish high school?"

"Well," replied Bill, "I was having trouble running the farm by myself and going to school full time too. You see, my father died a year ago October and my mother died last February, so it was pretty difficult keeping things going alone. When Aunt Anne and Uncle John offered to let me stay with them while I finished school, I jumped at the chance. I leased the farm to my Aunt Elsie and her husband for a dollar a year plus a share of any profits. They were able to hire a family to help work the farms since my house was available for someone else to use, so here I am."

"Oh my, you poor boy," exclaimed Margaret Stuart, "you lost both of your parents within a year?"

"Yes and I still think it's just a bad dream sometimes. But I really like my aunt and uncle, the school here is very good, and my part time job is giving me a chance to earn some money for college. So things could be a whole lot worse."

Just as Alex Stuart was opening his mouth to say something else, Allison rushed into the room and announced that they would have to run to catch the bus if they were going to get there on time. Hasty good-byes were exchanged and Allison's mother told Bill to be sure to come back to visit again soon.

The production of the "King and I" by the school drama department was incredibly good. The cast was truly professional in their performance and Allison and Bill were very impressed with the singing. The chance to hold hands and snuggle together during the show just added to their enjoyment. The time went by very quickly and before they knew it, they were outside in the cold night air on Broadway mingling with the crowd waiting for the bus to come.

As they stood close together at the bus stop, Bill felt Allison shudder for a moment, then turn towards him. "What's the matter, Allison," Bill said, alarmed. "What's wrong?"

"Someone I went out with once a long time ago is over there with a group of his friends. He's not very nice and is usually just hanging around looking for girls to go out with him after the football games. He's on the team and lets everyone know what a good player he is. I didn't expect to see him here tonight after a play."

"Don't worry about it, Allison. He's not going to bother us."

Bill had just finished speaking when Stan Warner pushed his way through the crowd to confront them. "Well, if it isn't miss uppity bitch out with the country bumpkin. What a sight! How did you sneak out without your old man catching you?"

Stan was a big guy, taller than Bill and much heavier. He really looked the part of a football player, even without the padding. Bill, in a low tone of voice, suggested that he return to his group of friends and leave them alone to wait for the bus in peace.

"Peace shit," said Stan shoving Bill backwards a couple of steps, "I'm going to take uppity bitch home tonight and show her what a real man is like." Bill warned him quietly that he was being offensive and told him to take off before he got himself into trouble. The boys in the group at the bus stop, sensing a fight about to begin, gathered around to watch the action as the girls moved farther away.

Stan grinned for a moment and then turned serious and lunged at Bill with his arm drawn back and his fist ready to flatten him. Bill, remembering well his police defensive tactics course, quickly leaned to one side, grabbed Stan's arm, and propelled him face down on the grass. He then dropped down with one knee in the small of Stan's back and twisted his arm up towards his neck, holding the pressure. He was in perfect position to put the cuffs on him, but of course he didn't have any.

"Oooow," screamed Stan, you're breaking my arm!"

"Not yet," replied Bill quietly, "but if you don't apologize to Allison and everyone else here, that is exactly what I'm going to do."

Stan, half-blubbering by this time, muttered an apology of

sorts. Bill made him repeat it in a loud voice to the crowd. Then, noticing that the bus had arrived and most people were already on it, he jumped up, took Allison by the hand and quickly boarded as the doors were closing. As the bus pulled away, they noticed Stan getting to his feet and rubbing his arm as he went over to rejoin his friends, who were beginning to laugh at him.

By the time they got off the Victoria bus and were walking towards Sixty-second Allison was herself again. Except that she snuggled closer to Bill than usual and let him take her all the way home. Bill thanked her again for going out with him and mentioned something about going to a movie one Saturday night. As they stood on the porch at the front door, he leaned over to kiss her cheek just as the door opened. Alex Stuart glared at him, suggested that Allison come inside and then firmly closed the door in his face. Bill went home happy anyway, as it really had turned out to be a pretty good evening.

✸
Twenty-six

Bill got off the night owl Number Twenty bus at 4:40 a.m. Friday morning and headed across the street to the warehouse complex. It was very cold and very dark, so he was grateful for the warmth as he entered the building and went to his locker. He got one of the new gray shirts off the shelf and changed into his uniform, then went to truck fifteen and waited for Chuck. Just after five, Chuck unlocked the truck doors and told Bill to arrange the boxes to be delivered into the correct order for the stops that they were going to make. Reviewing the delivery order lists, Bill slowly moved the heavy boxes around to make sure that the ones closest to the doors were the ones for the first stop. He was only half finished when Chuck came to the rear loading door and announced that it was time to close up and get going. Bill hastily moved one more box, then climbed down and secured both loading doors before getting into the cab beside Chuck. They pulled away from the dock at exactly 5:25 a.m.

The first stop on Chuck's route was still the Hotel Vancouver, so Bill was pleased to see his Uncle John when they went into the main kitchen to announce their arrival. Following the usual routine, Bill carried the boxes from the truck to the kitchen receiving area where John checked the contents against the order form as his staff put things away. While Bill continued to shuttle back and forth with the boxes, Chuck opened the cab safe and took out the special order bags. Bill caught a glimpse of him as he went down the hall to the lobby carrying the plastic bags and wondered what he was doing. Chuck had ample time to complete his business and go back to the receiving area before Bill finished, so he chatted with John for a minute or two and then took the order form for the next day's delivery. Checking his watch, he then quickly went back to the truck with Bill trotting along behind after lingering to say a hasty "good-bye."

The routine was the same for the rest of the morning, Bill unloaded the truck while Chuck delivered the special orders out of Bill's sight. On the trip back to the warehouse, Bill was determined to come up with a method where he could unload in time to see what Chuck was up to. At dinner that evening, Bill asked his uncle if he knew what Chuck did with the items that he took into the lobby. John said that he honestly had never noticed, since he was always intent on making sure that they received what was ordered and paid for. He agreed to keep an eye open without being too obvious, or alerting his staff to what he was doing. Bill went out to the drug store after dinner to use the pay phone and make a couple of small purchases. As he walked past Sixty-second Street on the way home, he regretted having to work on a school day because he couldn't see Allison after school as he usually did. He promised himself that he would phone her tomorrow after work to see if she could go to a movie with him.

The Saturday morning routine on the truck went much better. As soon as Bill got access to the truck at 5:00 a.m., he took a collection of colored marking pens out of his pocket and, without rearranging the boxes in order of delivery, he simply color coded them in order of unloading. Thus everything destined for the Hotel Vancouver had the order number highlighted in yellow, then blue for all the boxes for the next hotel, green for the third one and so on for all of the stops on the route. Consequently, he had the doors secured and was ready to go before Chuck could call him. Chuck looked at him a little strangely when he climbed into the cab, but didn't say anything. He also didn't notice that Bill was able to take a couple of breaks from the unloading activities to surreptitiously watch Chuck's routine. He even saw the process of opening the cab safe and the removal of the bags before locking it up again.

At the next stop, he was able to see Chuck return from the lobby and open the safe again, quickly putting a smaller bag inside. Bill worked even harder at the third stop and was finished in time to peek into the lobby area and see Chuck talking to the newsstand clerk as he received something from her in exchange for the last full bag. By the end of the workday on Saturday afternoon he had much more to report to his "E" Division contact. Chuck had told him that he was pleased to see how quickly Bill had adjusted to the routine on the truck and promised him that they would soon be taking some special trips. It was truck fifteen's turn in the rotation to make some of the longer out-of-town weekend deliveries.

Saturday evening, with her parent's mixed blessings, Bill and Allison took the bus downtown and went to a movie, then strolled up and down Robson Street enjoying the crowds and the excitement of Saturday night in the city. He had enjoyed the movie, more for the opportunity to put his arm around Allison and hold her close than the picture itself. He also enjoyed taking her for coffee and Danish in one of the many places on Robson where there was a live music group playing. Expensive, but fun. The real highlight though, came as they walked to her home after getting off the bus and paused under a tree for a little while just a block away from the house to exchange kisses and conversation.

On Sunday afternoon, Bill took his aunt on a bus trip to visit the gardens in Queen Elizabeth Park, which are beautiful at any time of the year. As they strolled through the sculpture garden admiring the lifelike art forms, an attractive young woman with blond hair, wearing designer jeans and an *I Love Vancouver* sweatshirt, rushed up to them.

"Mrs. Cassidy," she said, "how nice to see you again. You probably don't remember me. I'm Sarah Matthews. *Corporal Sarah Matthews, "E" Division,*" she whispered.

"Oh, hello Sarah, it's nice to see you again too," Anne replied reacting smoothly. "I would like you to meet my nephew, Bill Patterson. Since we're going in the same direction, why don't you walk along with us and we can chat a little bit."

As they wandered along and stopped periodically to admire different areas of the gardens, Bill quietly brought Sarah up to date on everything that he had observed so far while working on the truck route. Every now and then, Anne would interject to talk about old friends and keep Sarah engaged in conversation while Bill carefully studied the information about the various trees and shrubs in the garden as any good farmer would do.

Bill suggested to Sarah that division arrange for undercover surveillance of the hotel lobby areas all along the route during their delivery times each day, and get a few photos of Chuck's activities. This would allow Bill to perform his normal job without the danger of Chuck getting suspicious. Sarah agreed and said that if they saw what she suspected they would, they would start surveillance along all twenty-eight of the company's delivery routes.

Twenty-seven

Two weeks later, as Bill arrived at the truck early on Saturday morning, he was surprised to see Chuck already there waiting for him.

"Early start today," Chuck announced, "we're going to take the ferry to Vancouver Island this morning and do the Nanaimo area deliveries."

Bill had no time to sort his boxes in order of unloading since Chuck immediately checked the doors and then motioned Bill into the cab. They pulled out of the yard ahead of the other trucks and continued onto Hastings Street, Highway One, the Second Narrows Bridge, and along the Upper Levels Highway to the Horseshoe Bay Ferry Terminal. As they waited to board, Bill remarked to Chuck that he was really impressed with the scenery since he had never been through West Vancouver before. Chuck assured him that he hadn't seen anything yet; it got much better when seen from the ferry.

Bill thought that the designation of ferry was totally inadequate as they drove on board the ship and continued down the vehicle deck, which was very well lit and much bigger than the inside of any barn he had ever seen. Even the tractor-trailer trucks that came on board after them were dwarfed by the size of the ship's interior. The next area that impressed Bill was the restaurant, where he ordered the buffet breakfast and sat next to a picture window where the view was indeed magnificent. Chuck seemed immune to all this, but then he had traveled the route often. Bill had to pinch himself to believe that he was actually at work and getting paid for enjoying all of this.

During breakfast, Bill casually mentioned his surprise at having seen Mr. Salvatore and Mr. Sabatini in the warehouse at 5:00 a.m. yesterday morning. Chuck explained that every Friday and Saturday senior management traveled on weekly buying trips to various suppliers throughout BC, Alberta and Washington State. He said that often they would go into the plant early for a quick strategy meeting before going to the airport. Chuck also said that the reason things were more relaxed in the warehouse on Fridays and Saturdays was because senior management was away and the younger generation was running things. The Chairman, Mr. Battista, stayed in his office and didn't travel any more but he never bothered anyone unless some real crises occurred.

Just as Bill was trying to decide if he could safely ask more questions, the ship began the approach to the Departure Bay Terminal and it was time to return to the truck.

As the truck left the ramp and moved through the terminal, Chuck explained the route that they were going to follow, beginning with the hotels, resorts and restaurants on the outskirts of Nanaimo and finishing up in the heart of town about 1:00 p.m. Bill put in a hard morning's work since Chuck seemed intent on meeting a very tight schedule. This required keeping the unloading moving along at a very fast pace at each stop. Consequently, Bill was relieved to hear that the downtown Bastion Inn was the last stop and that lunch would be on the company when the unloading was completed.

Chuck moved the truck from the loading dock out into the parking lot as soon as Bill had finished unloading and secured the doors. He then escorted Bill inside through the main lobby door to the dining room where Chuck invited him to order whatever he wanted from the lunch menu. Bill didn't really want much despite his busy morning because he had really taken advantage of the breakfast buffet onboard the ferry. Halfway through the meal, he excused himself and headed for the men's room.

On the way back, for some unknown reason, he decided to have a look at the truck just to make sure that everything was okay. As he reached the glass door leading to the parking lot, he stopped in total amazement. A large gray SUV was parked right beside the truck with its tail gate wide open. The truck's side loading door, which Bill had carefully locked, was also wide open. Two well-dressed men were reaching into the SUV for something and as Bill continued to watch, they lifted out a large, full, heavy duffel bag, and heaved it into the truck. Bill had started to go out the door to see what was going on when he suddenly stopped in his tracks, then quickly moved back out of sight and prayed that he hadn't been seen. Mr. Dominic Salvatore and Mr. John Sabatini, senior company executives, proceeded to move three more duffel bags from the SUV into the truck. As Bill peeked around the doorframe, he saw them close and lock the truck door then close up the SUV and drive away.

As he returned to the table and sat down Chuck looked at him closely, suspecting that something wasn't quite right. Bill apologized for being away so long and said that something he ate for breakfast had been bothering him but he felt better now. Chuck looked at his watch and said that they would leave for the ferry in about thirty minutes, so if Bill wanted coffee or a coke he should order it now. Bill asked what ferry they would be getting and Chuck indicated that the 3:00 p.m. was the one he usually caught because he liked to coordinate his schedule with the one for the northern Gulf Island routes. Bill expressed curiosity about the coordination with ferry schedules and Chuck explained that if you went to the terminal after the northern ferry routes traffic had already boarded and left for Horseshoe Bay, then the next ferries were not as crowded.

The trip back to Vancouver was uneventful, except for the surprising offer that Chuck had for Bill. If he was willing to work on Sunday next week, he could accompany Chuck to California on the weekly trip to pick up fresh citrus fruit and grapes. They would leave early next Friday morning and return Sunday night. Bill could expect to share in the driving since they would spend a lot of time on the road. Bill jumped at the chance, since he had never been to California and; of course, he wanted to see what kind of business was really conducted on a trip like that. They rolled into the company warehouse complex just before 6:00 p.m. Saturday evening, and Chuck reminded Bill to bring his driver's license and passport with him for the trip next Friday.

On Sunday morning the late March weather was beautiful, sunny and warm with the daffodils in full bloom. Allison and Bill went to church together for the first time, walking from her house to the neighborhood parish church. The liturgy was upbeat and the sermon positive, extolling the love of God for everyone, saint and sinner alike. They left the mass buoyed up, confident and very hungry, so they went to a nearby restaurant for breakfast. Bill sprung his idea on Allison during their second cup of coffee. Since graduation was in sight and the workload was getting heavier, why not go home, get their book bags, and take the bus to Stanley Park. They could find a picnic table in a quiet area and do their homework together while they enjoyed the spring weather. Allison was all for it, so they went to her house first, told Mrs. Stuart about their plans and headed out the door before Sergeant Stuart knew what was going on. They had a wonderful day, got lots of work done and spent a lot of time expressing their love for each other. On the way home, Bill couldn't help but think about how he was going to explain to Allison who he really was, after the case had been broken, which; if all went well, was now likely to happen right around graduation time.

✸ Twenty-eight

Friday morning was wet and windy, typical March weather as Bill arrived at work carrying an overnight bag that Uncle John had loaned him. He didn't care about the weather though, since he was excited at the prospect of going to California. Chuck arrived five minutes after he did and they checked the truck together to make sure that it was empty, clean, and ready for the long trip. Once again they got underway before the other trucks began to roll out of the yard and headed south to Marine Drive continuing on to Highway Ninety-nine and the border crossing. They drove over to Highway 15 to the Pacific Highway Truck Crossing.

At the border crossing, since they were empty and all of the truck's paperwork was in order, they breezed through the US Customs and Immigration inspections and headed south on Interstate Five. After driving for just over three hours, south through Seattle and Olympia, they stopped near Tumwater and had breakfast. After breakfast, Chuck informed Bill that it was time he earned his keep and tossed the keys to him. Bill was thrilled and eager to demonstrate his driving prowess, so he eagerly accepted the challenge and eased the big vehicle out of the parking lot, down the highway, and back onto I-5.

The next twelve hours were uneventful as they continued

south, alternately driving or dozing in the passenger seat as they rolled along the interstate just over the posted speed limit. As they neared Sacramento, Chuck woke Bill up and asked him to start watching for highway signs. They had to leave I-5 at Highway 113 and continue south through Davis to I-80 and then south again on Highway 113 through Dixon. As Chuck was moving onto the ramp from I-80 to 113, he ran through the remains of a truck tire that had suffered a blowout at high speed. They couldn't avoid the strands of steel from the belted radial since there was no room on the ramp to drive around the debris and inevitably just south of Dixon, the telltale bumps and vibrations of a flat front tire were felt.

Swearing mightily, Chuck managed to bring the truck to a stop safely and Bill, eager to help, had the door open ready to get out and change the tire. Chuck grabbed him and told him that the spare could not be used. Bill argued, saying that when he checked it this morning in its stowed position under the rear door-loading ramp it looked okay.

Chuck told him again that the tire was no good; it had a weak sidewall and said that he was going to phone the company orchard near Elmira to tell them to bring out a spare tire. He told Bill that they had several tires and rims at the farm which would fit the truck. He also told Bill to stay where he was, then got out to make a call on his cellular phone. Bill knew that Chuck could easily have called while sitting in the cab and strained to hear what was being said but wasn't able to distinguish anything above the background noise of passing traffic.

Twenty minutes later, a pickup truck with two tough looking farm hands arrived with a spare wheel. After perfunctory introductions were exchanged, Bill and Chuck watched as they rapidly jacked up the truck and replaced the front tire. The also removed the spare from under the truck and replaced it with a new one. Lifting the heavy wheels into the back of the pickup, they then headed off down the road to the farm as Chuck followed far behind. Bill was impressed with the little that he saw in the gathering darkness as they rolled passed miles of citrus orchards, many with roadside stands offering freshly picked fruit. They finally turned into a long driveway, which led eventually to a sprawling old farmhouse surrounded by barns and produce storage sheds.

Chuck pulled the truck into a parking area near the house and then led Bill inside to meet the farm foreman and some of his crew. They immediately became aware of the smell of dinner cooking and realized just how hungry they were, since they only ate snacks off and on since breakfast. The housekeeper ushered them into the dining room while the foreman explained that all they had to do was relax now since his crew would service and load the truck for their early morning departure.

After dinner, Bill was shown to his room at the far end of the house. Looking out the window before putting the light on, he saw that he had a marvelous view of the barn and its open door. The place looked more like a workshop than a barn and it was not only lit up but a beehive of activity. Some of the people he had seen at dinner were now working in the shop. In addition to a long bench and storage cupboards, there was one of those bulky machines which removed tires from wheel rims.

As he watched from behind the curtain, he saw them drag in a wheel with a flat tire, which he assumed had come from their truck. They skillfully removed the old tire and mounted a new one very quickly. Then they rolled in another wheel with what seemed to be a pretty good tire and very carefully removed it from the wheel. As one man mounted a new tire, the others lifted the old tire onto the bench and proceeded to remove dozens of plastic bags from inside the tire. They weighed each bag and then stored them in a cupboard.

The realization slowly came to Bill that the bags were coming out of the truck's spare tire, which certainly explained why Chuck was so adamant about not using it when they needed it the most. He also realized now why an orchard would stock spare truck tires and wheels. With a sick feeling, Bill realized that they had just imported drugs into the United States when he had been fully expecting that they would have been taking them back into Canada with the cargo. At this point he decided that he had better be visible to Chuck, so he hurried back to the lounge and joined the few people sitting in front of the TV set.

The trip back to Vancouver started out badly then got progressively worse. It became obvious immediately that this remote part of the company operation didn't have the skilled loading crews that QHRS headquarters had. The scheduled 5:30 a.m. departure was closer to 10:00 a.m. and only then because Bill and Chuck completed the loading. Bill initially had to unload half of what was already onboard to stow it properly, otherwise they would not have had room for a full cargo to carry back. Once underway they ran into a lot of Saturday morning traffic on the way to I-5, which delayed them even more and with the full load there wasn't much power available to pass automobiles. Even worse, the weight really slowed them down when climbing the hills once they got into mountain country. The heavy rains began as they approached Mount Shasta.

By the time it began to get dark, Chuck had enough. He pulled off into a truck stop near Chehalis, Washington and announced that they would spend the night at the motel and get an early start in the morning. That suited Bill just fine since he wanted to phone Allison and see how her weekend had been so far. That didn't work either, since Sergeant Stuart curtly informed him that Allison was out shopping with her mother. Bill and Chuck had an early dinner in the restaurant then turned in, hoping for a smoother trip tomorrow.

Sunday morning was cloudy and windy, but the rain had stopped as they got underway at six. The next few hours went well and they arrived at the Pacific Truck Crossing just before ten. As they moved along slowly in the commercial truck line inching towards the Customs and Immigration inspectors, Chuck got the cargo manifests arranged in the correct order, had the truck registration and insurance papers ready, and made sure that Bill had his driver's license and passport available.

The Immigration Officer welcomed them, checked their IDs, and then waved them on to Customs. The Customs Officer perfunctorily glanced at the paperwork, glared at the two of them, and then curtly ordered them to pull into the truck inspection lot. Chuck immediately felt doomed, knowing full well that this could cost them an hour or more of wasted time when he was anxious to get home to the family for what was left of the weekend.

Customs Officer Arnold Douglas was suspicious of this lot, an older driver, a young punk helper who didn't look old enough to hold down a full time job and a Vancouver truck with a load of produce from California. Sure. He had the dog handler give the outside of the truck, the engine compartment and the underside of the chassis a thorough going over while he carefully studied the manifests. Nothing. So he ordered that the cargo be unloaded for inspection.

Chuck immediately protested and reminded Douglas that they had perishable cargo that needed to be delivered to the Vancouver warehouse as soon as possible to maintain freshness. Bullshit. He carefully watched as every box and crate was unloaded, inspected, and sniffed by the dog. Then the inside of the truck was gone over inch by thorough inch, nothing.

He next ordered Chuck and Bill to go inside the office. Chuck really protested this time, and said that they would go in only after they had reloaded the cargo and locked the truck. With a grudging okay, Chuck and Bill were sent to separate inspection rooms and Bill received the first visit from Customs Officer Douglas. He was told to empty his pockets completely and put everything, including his U.S. purchases, on the table. He was then told to stand still while Douglas carefully looked over everything, including the contents of his wallet. The stuffed animal with the *"I♥California"* patch that Bill had purchased for Allison was ripped open and the stuffing carefully examined. Next, Bill was told to remove his clothing, everything except his undershorts.

Bill obeyed slowly, knowing that legally he couldn't refuse. The inspector then examined every pocket, cuff and seam. When nothing was found, Douglas made a big show of opening the cupboard and removing a pair of rubber gloves and a tube of lubricant. He informed Bill that this was his last chance to declare any contraband before a body cavity search was conducted. Bill by this time was absolutely fuming, but could do nothing without jeopardizing his cover. As he was ordered to remove his underwear he suddenly remembered a legal point and demanded that a customs supervisor be brought in to witness this part of the search. This demand caused Douglas to pause and then slowly pick up Bill's wallet again. "Tell you what I'll do for you punk. I'll just relieve you of this left over American cash and you can be on your way."

Bill was overjoyed; he was now fully justified in arresting the son-of-a-bitch for extortion. Except that under the present circumstances of his undercover assignment, he wasn't in a position to do it. He would surely remember Customs Officer Douglas for a long, long time though. Bill waited beside the truck until Chuck came out, white with fury. He intended to make a full report to company management and ask them to have the government do something about this kind of harassment of company employees. They continued the trip home in silence and were both very happy to turn into the QHRS complex, back into the loading bay and turn the truck over to the extremely efficient guys in the green shirts to do the unloading.

Bill and Allison had a lot to talk about over lunch at school the next day. He described the whole trip from beginning to end, except for a few irrelevant details. He gave her the illustrated books on the Napa Valley wine country and the citrus groves of Southern California, and they mourned together over the fate of the late stuffed animal. Things got considerably more cheerful though as they discussed graduation just a couple of months away and the social activities being planned after the finals were over. They even tentatively talked about their personal post-graduation plans as a couple, although Bill of necessity had to be a little vague about his future college plans.

✦ Twenty-nine

The bright April morning sun was coming into the bedroom through a small gap in the drapes and was shining into the eyes of the sleeper. With a sigh, Sergeant Ben Thundercloud, NCOIC of the White Rock Detachment, rolled over and looked at the clock. He had been enjoying the luxury of a sleep-in on his day off and was pleasantly surprised to see that it was just after 8:00 a.m., which was a hell of a lot better than the usual noisy alarm going off in his ear at 5:30 a.m. He relaxed for a few minutes more, then got up and made his way into the bathroom. After a sloppy shave and a hot shower he emerged and began to carefully make selections from his extensive wardrobe to select what would be most suitable for an adventurous day in the sun. He first chose a somewhat grubby, wrinkled, T-shirt with a slightly obscene verse on the front. He then carefully matched it with a pair of faded jeans with a hole in one knee and one rear pocket partially torn off. Next, he selected a greasy baseball cap, which, when worn backwards, displayed to the world a logo extolling the virtues of Harley-Davidson machines. Quite satisfied with his appearance in the mirror, he proceeded out the back door and went down the lane to the impound lot where he chose a dented pick-up truck with a freshly painted front fender which almost matched the rest of the bright red paint.

As the engine roared to life, he paused to select a loud heavy-metal rock station on the FM radio and then pulled onto the highway heading for the U.S. border. As he approached U.S. Customs and Immigration, he turned off the radio and removed his cap. When he got to the booth, he had his wallet open and his RCMP identification card ready for inspection. In response to the quizzical look from the inspector, he admitted that when he was off duty on a spring Sunday morning he liked to get away from the area where he had jurisdiction. This way he could enjoy some time to himself where the citizens wouldn't recognize him and provide free advice on how the force should conduct its business. He got a knowing grin in return and was told to enjoy his day.

When he turned off I-5 in Bellingham, he proceeded towards the bay until he spotted a restaurant with an outside seating area. He then parked, walked in and sat down to a leisurely breakfast while reading the local newspaper. When he finished an hour later, he paid with a large denomination bill and asked for his change in one-dollar bills. Later as he strolled around town, he made stops to buy magazines and candy bars and again made sure that he received many one-dollar bills in change. After a half-hour or so of reading and relaxation in a park overlooking the water, he strolled back to the truck and headed towards I-5 North.

As he approached the Canada Customs lanes at the Pacific Truck Crossing, he put on his cap and turned up the radio. Then he entered the lane for commercial vehicles only, creeping slowly ahead behind the line of tractor trailers as he awkwardly slid a wide plastic bag down the back of his trousers and into his underwear. When he reached the immigration officer, he turned down the radio and produced his photo driver's license for inspection. After answering the usual questions about his place of residence and the amount of time spent out of the country, he was told to move ahead to the customs area.

With the radio turned up again and his small purchases in a bag beside him on the front seat, he winked at the customs officer and wished him a good day. The custom's inspector was not amused at all and gruffly questioned him about the value of his purchases and demanded details of anything else that he might have to declare. He then ordered Ben to pull into the inspection lot. Once there he told Ben to get out of the truck so that it could be searched, but to turn that frigging radio off first. Ben cheerfully complied and opened both truck doors and lifted the hood to demonstrate his cooperation. The inspector was not appreciative. The truck was searched very carefully while Ben continued to watch with amusement . . . nothing.

Ben was then ordered to bring his purchases and follow the customs inspector into the office for more detailed questioning. After reiterating loudly that he had nothing of value to declare, he was ordered into an examination room. The other customs officials' working inside the office paid absolutely no attention to what was going on until, about five minutes later, the door to the examination room was suddenly flung open and Customs Officer Arnold Douglas was shoved through it with his hands cuffed behind his back. He was followed seconds later by Ben, who took a firm grip on Douglas's upper arm and held him in the middle of the room.

"I am Sergeant Benjamin Thundercloud, Royal Canadian Mounted Police," he proclaimed, "This man is under arrest. Please call 911 and ask the dispatcher to send a patrol unit to transport a prisoner." A customs supervisor bustled up and brusquely demanded some identification which Ben promptly produced. The supervisor, somewhat deflated, turned away and picked up the telephone.

Inside the room Ben had been told to empty his pockets

and remove everything from his paper bag for inspection. No argument from Ben. The inspector picked up his bulging wallet and looked appreciatively inside. Ben was then told that he was suspected of concealing contraband and was ordered to remove his clothing for a more intimate search. Ben smiled and told the inspector that if he had known about this routine, he would have worn his dirtiest underwear. No sense of humor.

After examining Ben's clothing with obvious disgust, the inspector announced that Ben had two choices, he could submit to a body cavity search or he could forfeit his U.S. cash. Ben calmly announced that there was really a third choice and pulled the plastic bag from the back of his underpants. The inspector immediately snatched the bag out of his hand and reached inside, pulling out the nylon handcuffs first without realizing what they were and then the RCMP identification card, which he read before blanching and beginning to stutter an apology. After the constable had put Douglas in the back of the patrol vehicle and headed out to the highway, Ben strolled over to the truck and climbed in. He threw the ball cap onto the ledge behind the seat and started the engine. Next, he found an oldies station on the radio and moved on up the road to go home, hoping that the rest of his day off would be as much fun as the first half had been.

Part III

The Bottom Line

Thirty

Sal Battista was not a happy man. He had just completed another grueling Friday in the special orders department and was tired. But more than tired, he was depressed. He wasn't afraid of hard work, in fact he had enjoyed his first two years with the company working with the loading crews and especially working as a crew chief, because there he was an integral part of the operations of the great company that his great-great -grandfather had co-founded so long ago. The principal part of the business as a quality wholesale food distributor really appealed to him, but the ever-growing special orders department did not. Sure it was incredibly profitable; allowing family members of all the different generations to live like royalty, but it was also completely illegal and was contributing to the downfall of young people throughout the entire region. Worse than that, it had become a power trip for upper management who thought that they were invulnerable and profits would increase forever. It was only the total dedication of a few senior employees that kept the basic business performing so successfully.

To make matters worse, Sal had nobody to discuss his fears and concerns with. He certainly couldn't talk to his young wife about it, she was totally absorbed in caring for their new child and felt very secure in the knowledge that Sal would be part of the senior management team one day. He certainly couldn't voice his concerns to other family members, they would have him killed if they sensed any disloyalty. You could not resign from QHRS if you were aware of the inside structure of the company.

As he continued walking through the warehouse and past the employee lunchroom on his way to the door leading to the parking lot, a possible solution physically struck him. Tall, lanky, and ever cheerful Bill Patterson, who was walking in one direction while talking and looking in another, came out of the lunchroom and ran right into him. After apologizing profusely to Sal, Bill said goodbye to the fellow driver's helper he had been talking to and then asked Sal how he was doing with his new job. This made Sal realize that there may indeed be an outsider that he could talk to safely. He liked Bill and trusted him despite his youth. He seemed to have a mature outlook far beyond that of a typical high school senior.

Acting on a whim, Sal invited Bill and his girlfriend to dinner on Sunday evening, offering the opportunity to see the new baby and meet his wife, Cheryl. Nothing fancy, just salad, a pasta dish and good California wine after the Sunday evening mass, which Sal wanted to attend since he was scheduled to work on Sunday morning. Bill accepted immediately, hoping that Allison would agree, because he genuinely liked his former supervisor and of course he was always looking for an opportunity to spend more time with Allison.

Promptly at six Sunday evening, Bill and Allison rang the bell at the Battista residence and waited as they heard an infant crying inside. Bill had not had any trouble persuading Allison to go out to the dinner with him; and surprisingly, her father had voiced no objection. He had become much friendlier towards Bill lately. Of course, no one was aware that Detective Sergeant Stuart had done what he had promised his wife he would not do, checked the computer at police headquarters to see if there was a file on Bill. He had even gone so far as to phone the RCMP Fairview Detachment to see if Bill had any record as a troublemaker. Sergeant Stuart was pleasantly surprised when the Duty Constable, Cy Perkins, had praised Bill as an outstanding young man just before seriously grilling him as to what his interest in Mr. Patterson might be. He had seemed relieved when the true reason for the inquiry was revealed.

Cheryl opened the door and welcomed them, apologizing for keeping them waiting at the door while they changed the baby. Sal appeared behind her and immediately ushered them into the living room while Cheryl disappeared into the kitchen. After formally meeting Sal, Allison joined Cheryl in the kitchen so that she could see little Margo in the playpen and talk to her while dinner was being dished up. After a delightful dinner with much laughter and story telling, Cheryl and Allison disappeared to feed the baby and get her ready for bed while Sal and Bill moved into the kitchen to clean up.

As Sal washed the pots and pans and passed them to Bill to be dried, he suddenly stopped what he was doing and turned towards Bill. "Can you keep something I tell you in strict confidence?" Sal asked Bill in a low voice, "There are things going on within the company that I'm really unhappy about and I can't discuss them with anyone in my family." Bill turned serious immediately and assured Sal that anything he heard would be just between them unless Sal agreed otherwise.

"Bill, there are segments of the company's operations, particularly in the special orders department, that are highly profitable but extremely illegal and I'm afraid that sooner or later they're going to bring down the entire company. I can't discuss them with management, not even my father or grandfather, without putting Cheryl and myself in danger, not to mention the risk to the baby. Does your Uncle John have any friends in law enforcement that I could safely talk to?"

Bill stood in shocked silence. *Now this is interesting,* he thought, *does he seriously want to talk to someone or is he suspicious of me and is using this as a test?* Bill decided that he had to be very cool about this and reveal no more than was absolutely necessary until he learned more about his motives. "My uncle has a lot of close friends in town," Bill said, "and some of them are well connected in law enforcement. The problem is that I don't know how to set up a meeting so you can talk privately to the right people without arousing a lot of suspicion as to how you met these new friends. You might be better off relaying your concerns through me, since no one will be aware of whom my uncle brings to the house for a visit." Sal thought about that for a minute.

"Bill, I'm going to trust my life to you. When the circumstances are right and you have a good contact through your uncle, I'll relay what's going on. But please understand, that

this is serious stuff and could result in you, me, my wife and child being in extreme danger if word ever got out. Even Allison could be threatened by association."

Just then, Cheryl and Allison brought the baby in to say "goodnight" to everyone, so naturally everyone had to troop into the nursery to participate in the night-night ceremony. Later, when they were settled in the living room, Allison announced to Bill that they were going to baby-sit next Saturday night so that Sal and Cheryl could go out to dinner and a movie for the first time in months. Bill enthusiastically agreed and said that they might even get a chance to study for their finals while they were there.

As they were saying their "goodbyes" and getting ready for the walk back to the bus stop, Bill managed to tell Sal that he would have information for him on a safe contact by Saturday when they returned. Sal gave him the thumbs up sign and wished them a safe trip home.

Thirty-one

Anne Cassidy drove Bill half way around the west side of Vancouver to make sure that they were not being followed and then dropped him off a block away from "E" Division headquarters. Bill watched carefully for anyone who might be paying attention to where he was going as he approached the building, then scurried around to the back to an entrance door near the parking lot. He knocked once and the door opened immediately. After producing his identification card which was carefully scrutinized, he was warmly welcomed.

"Greetings, I'm Don Zimmerman," the uniformed constable said. "I'm one of your telephone contacts. And this is Corporal Matthews, my boss and yours too, but of course you didn't know that. I'm sure that you recognize her from your visit to the park. You know something else Bill, you really don't look old enough to be a member of the force."

Bill was really pleased to meet other members of the team, and was appreciative of the warm welcome. This was his first contact with serving members since leaving "Depot Division" and he was happy to be treated as an equal. They got right down to business though and immediately led him to the general investigation section conference room where he was introduced to Chief Superintendent Singh, Inspector Janice Marshall,

Inspector Doug Crenshaw of Drug Enforcement, Inspector Mike Hanley of the Island District CID and Staff Sergeant Colin McPherson.

Bill was thoroughly intimidated by the presence of all the commissioned officers in the room and began to feel like a schoolboy in the presence of the principal and the entire teaching staff. Corporal Matthews told him to relax and reminded him that he was a valuable member of the investigating team. The chief superintendent reiterated what she had just said and apologized for asking him to come in at some risk to his cover, but also explained that the investigation was reaching a critical point where action must soon be taken. This latest information that he had found a potential inside informant was so valuable that it warranted a personal report to the entire team.

Bill, remembering his cadet training, gave a concise verbal report of all of his observations from a company employee's perspective, providing details of what he had seen and had been told, but leaving out any speculation. All of his remarks and his answers to questions focused strictly on the facts. During his report, there were confirming nods and affirming remarks as he led the room through his QHRS career. The background information he provided about Sal and his seemingly genuine concern for his future and that of the company struck a responsive note.

At this point, Inspector Crenshaw began a series of questions about the warehouse, its layout, security, and the number of employees on the premises at various times during the workweek. Bill drew a detailed layout of the buildings on the blackboard, providing the interior arrangements for all of the areas that he had been in. He was, unfortunately, unable to give any details of the interior of the special orders department complex or of the third floor executive suites. Everyone agreed that if Bill's contact was genuine, information about access and the security in place for the special orders department was of the utmost importance. Bill promised to pursue this with Sal, if there were guarantees of future protection for Sal and his family. Chief Superintendent Singh agreed that if Sal was a beneficial informant, all necessary protection would be provided.

Much discussion then took place on the timing of a raid. Doug Crenshaw wanted to plan for a raid within two weeks, but Mike Hanley strenuously objected, reminding everyone that he had a murder case to solve and the key to it was probably linked to the QHRS drug importing operations. He had to be sure that his suspects were active in the illicit Vancouver Island part of the operations before the company itself was raided. Bill advised them that a late Saturday evening timeframe would be the best for a raid, since there were no trucks making deliveries on Sunday mornings and because of that, no loading crews would be working in the warehouse on a Saturday evening. However, the maximum number of people would be in the special orders department that night, since this was the time of the week that the largest quantity of imported drugs would be going through the processing procedure.

Everyone agreed with this analysis and it was determined that details of the whole operation would be worked out within the next two or three weeks. Team leaders and support personnel would then be selected and trained with the entire team being put on standby each Saturday after training until Mike's intelligence came up with the right timeframe to initiate the operation. In the meantime, Bill was to concentrate on developing his informant and provide information through his telephone reports. He was not to take any chances or try to obtain any more information through his regular job activities.

Inspector Marshall talked about the large number of personnel that would be needed. It was obvious that assistance would be necessary from all of the large nearby detachments such as Burnaby and Surrey as well as from the Vancouver City Police. In addition, to support Mike's part of the operation on Vancouver Island, personnel from Courtenay, Campbell River and Nanaimo would be necessary. Air and marine resources would also be required. Secrecy was essential, but would be very difficult to maintain for long with an operation this large.

Inspector Crenshaw once again remarked on the necessity of conducting the raid quickly and shutting down the operation, including padlocking the entire complex, to reduce the flow of drugs into the region. Bill immediately objected and drew a withering look from the inspector.

"What's the matter constable, don't you want to bust your new found friends?"

"That's not the problem sir," Bill said getting to his feet, "If we shut down more than the special orders part of the operation, the entire hotel and restaurant industry in the region will be severely affected. If the trucks don't roll on a Monday morning with all of the food supplies that have been ordered, there will be serious repercussions since there is no readily available alternate source for the quantities required everyday in the city and for the resupply of the cruise ships."

Inspector Hanley immediately agreed. Turning to Chief Superintendent Singh, he said that it really would be necessary to obtain replacement truck drivers and put a new management team in place to resume normal business operations right away, even if it meant using police personnel temporarily. "Since you have the most business and financial experience inspector, does that mean you are volunteering?" asked the chief superintendent.

"Yes Sir," replied Mike, "if that's what it would take. Of course I would need Constable Patterson to run the warehouse for me and act as an advisor."

The chief superintendent told Inspector Marshall to include that aspect in the planning details. Shortly after that the meeting broke up on a friendly note and people began to file out of the room. Bill, to his dismay, suddenly realized that he had no easy way to get home. He quickly asked if someone could take him to a bus stop and Inspector Hanley, who was not in uniform, agreed to give him a ride.

Bill waited just inside the back door of the building until a sporty red Buick Lacrosse pulled up and then he scurried out and got into the passenger seat. Inspector Hanley, while telling him about some of his own undercover adventures, drove him on a very roundabout route to the Marpole Loop where he was able to catch a bus for the long ride home. On the way to the bus terminal, Mike complimented Bill on his presentation and reminded him that if the division did have to take over the QHRS management functions temporarily, he really would be a vital part of the continuing operations.

⛭

Thirty-two

Bill arrived at Sal and Cheryl's front door just a few minutes after Allison. Bill had gone home from work, showered and changed, then caught the bus to Sal's house. This was a whole lot easier than explaining to Allison's parents about their babysitting together when Sal came to pick up Allison. As Cheryl was explaining the baby's evening routine, Bill managed to take Sal aside for a minute and tell him that he had arranged a good confidential contact with an RCMP friend of his uncle if there was still an interest. Bill said once again that it would be best if Sal conveyed information through him to the contact, so that there would be absolutely no danger of Sal being discovered talking to anyone he had not previously known. Sal looked thoughtful and said that they could discuss it more when he took them home later on.

After Sal and Cheryl had left, Bill bustled around in the kitchen getting out the eggs, bacon and a biscuit mix since Cheryl had invited them to help themselves to anything they wanted to eat. Bill had not eaten since his early lunch and was getting pretty hungry by this time. Allison watched with interest as Bill expertly cracked the eggs for scrambling, put on the bacon and started mixing up the biscuit mix. He reminded Allison that he had lived alone on the farm for awhile and knew a little bit about cooking.

While Allison checked on Margo, who was laying in the playpen cooing away quite happily, Bill finished his work and served up two heaping plates of early evening breakfast delights.

As they ate they talked about their plans for graduation week, which party invitations they would accept and which ones to avoid. They agreed on which couples to sit with at the prom, and decided not to stay out all night even if their friends begged them to. Bill mentioned again that he was seriously worried about the finals, since with his job activities he hadn't been studying nearly enough. Allison reminded him that they had their books with them, so as soon as he finished the dishes they could start work. They also talked about summer jobs and college plans. Allison had been accepted at Simon Fraser University but Bill said that he just couldn't make up his mind between college and putting in an application at the police department. At least he didn't have to look for a summer job since he could easily work full time at QHRS during the vacation season.

After what seemed like just a few minutes of quiet studying at the kitchen table, Allison announced that it was time to put Margo to bed for the night. Bill cleaned up the kitchen and then helped her with the bath and playtime rituals watching in loving awe as Allison sat in the rocking chair softly singing lullabies as she held the sleepy baby. He could easily imagine that this was his own happy family and could genuinely feel how concerned Sal must be about the serious position he and his loved ones were in. When the baby was sound asleep, Allison gently put her down in the crib and they tiptoed out of the room.

Bill and Allison alternated between serious study periods and cuddling on the couch while watching TV, with the cuddling periods gradually becoming much longer than the study time. As they cuddled and kissed, they began to discuss their future and Bill made it clear that he had ruled out a military career and wanted to stay in the Vancouver region near Allison. Allison, on her part, said that she would go wherever Bill went if he would have her. Bill said that once graduation was behind them, they could get into some serious planning. Then they must have dozed off because the sound of the front door being opened and voices calling out brought them suddenly to their feet to greet Sal and Cheryl.

On the drive home Sal first went to Allison's house, walked her up to the front door, then returned to drive Bill the few blocks to his home. This gave Bill the opportunity for more discussion about a police contact. Sal said that with so much at stake, he just had to meet the primary person involved before he revealed very much. He had to be absolutely sure that the protection his family needed would be there. Bill agreed to talk to his uncle and come up with a plan whereby a safe introduction could be made.

Thirty-three

The large crowd was truly enjoying the traditional Saturday evening dinner dance orchestra in the hotel ballroom. The music wasn't too loud with a large variety of songs to suit the wide variation in age of the couples on the dance floor. At a table for four in a quiet corner of the room, not to far from the kitchen entrance, sat two couples that looked far too young to be out on their own, never mind having a baby with them. Margo sat quite happily in her car seat and watched the people swaying to the music across the room. There was a bit of a concern when Bill Patterson ordered some wine for the table and the waiter had impatiently demanded identification. Bill then took him aside near the kitchen door, showed him his ID, and explained that they were the guests of the executive chef, who happened to be his uncle. After that, the service and the food were absolutely superb.

Later in the evening, the couples took turns dancing and looking after the baby, who was still quite content. Just as they were thinking of going home so that they could get poor Margo to bed, a couple about ten years older came over to them from the dance floor.

"Hello there Bill, I'm Mike Hanley. Your uncle said that you might be here tonight. This is my wife Susan and we do hope that everyone is having a nice time."

Bill jumped up, almost knocking his chair over in the process and introduced everyone to Mr. and Mrs. Hanley, who insisted on being called Mike and Susan. Bill and Sal dragged two chairs over from a nearby table so that everyone could sit down and Mike very effectively entered into his role as an assistant hotel manager eager to chat about the band and ensure that everything was satisfactory. After just a few minutes of conversation, Susan noted that the baby had gone to sleep and probably should be on her way home. She invited everyone to her parent's house for Sunday brunch the next afternoon so that they could talk some more while enjoying the view of the ocean. She insisted that Margo come too, since she didn't have any children of her own yet and really wanted to enjoy a playful visit. After Bill gave a slight nod to Sal, he enthusiastically accepted the invitation on behalf of everybody at the table. Mike carefully gave travel directions to Sal, then everyone cheerfully said goodnight.

At another table, on the far side of the room, two members of the Sabatini family noted that young Sal was becoming far to friendly with that Patterson punk and his female friend. After all, he was just a driver's helper and not even a family member. Better keep an eye on that situation.

Sunday morning was sunny and mild with lots of late spring flowers in bloom when Sal, Cheryl, Margo and Allison drove up to the tidy house on Fifty-eighth Avenue where Bill was waiting on the porch. They set out for the Second Narrows Bridge and continued along the Upper Levels Highway to West Vancouver. Getting off the freeway, Sal proceeded to follow the directions that Mike had written out for him the night before. As they continued into British Properties, Allison and Cheryl both became nervous as the homes got bigger and the sea view more spectacular. Finally, Cheryl urged Sal to stop and carefully check the directions since she was convinced that they must be in the wrong neighborhood. Bill doubled checked the directions and saw that Sal was correct, but he was concerned himself that this area of very expensive homes wasn't the right place to be.

Sal bravely continued up the hill and cautiously turned into the driveway marked with the wrought iron house numbers corresponding with the directions. As they rolled to a stop in front of the four-car garage, Bill volunteered to see if this was indeed the right place while the others waited in the car. He rang the bell and then tried to think of an appropriate excuse for disturbing the occupants who couldn't possible be the Hanley's. Not even a commissioned officer could afford a place like this. The front door suddenly swung open and a smiling Susan stood in front of him.

"Hi, welcome to my parent's place, they're in Hawaii on vacation" she said. "You can get the rest of the crowd out of the car now. Mike and I have been watching and wondering if someone would be brave enough to come up to the door to see if the directions were right or not. It's a good thing for you, Constable Patterson, that you didn't make poor Allison come up to the door to see if you were at the right house!"

With that, she ran out to the car to welcome everyone and lead them into the house. Mike got everyone settled into the family room with a large Mimosa to drink and invited them to relax while Susan put the final touches on brunch. He knew, of course, that Allison and Cheryl would immediately get up and offer to help Susan in the kitchen so he was able to formally introduce himself to Sal as Inspector Hanley, Royal Canadian Mounted Police and indicated that they would have time to talk more after everyone ate.

The group divided themselves up in the traditional manner after a delightful meal on the patio, the women taking Margo off to be changed and put down for a nap while the men poured more coffee and started to talk about the hockey finals. Sal quietly began to ask Mike what assurances there were that his family would be protected if he shared the information that he so desperately needed to share. He also asked Mike if he thought that Bill should be part of the sensitive discussions. Mike wasn't ready to reveal Bill's true role in life just yet, so he just assured Sal that he knew Bill and his family more than well enough to be sure that he would keep everything that he heard in strict confidence.

As it turned out, Bill thought it best if he joined the women on a tour of the gardens around the house so that Mike and Sal would have more time to talk in private before the wives caught on that they were being left out of something. Mike gradually drew Sal out as his confidence increased and learned that the special orders operation was much bigger than anyone had dreamed of, with ties to many subsidiary businesses including Mike and Susan's previous employer, South American Shipping and Transportation Company and also a large operation in Chile.

Mike also learned that the security of the special orders department complex in the warehouse building was much tougher than anyone had planned on. The few access doors were steel plate, controlled with cipher locks, and monitored from both sides with video cameras. Interior walls were also steel, as was the special direct stair tower from the ground floor complex up to the executive suite on the third floor. The emergency doors leading to the outside were also of steel construction, as were the doors at each end of the escape tunnel to the maintenance garage. The inside lobby was guarded twenty-four hours a day with the video monitors mounted above the guard desk just inside the door. All senior employees inside the special orders laboratories, the cash room and the drug storage and packaging rooms were armed, as were all members of management when on duty. Even Sal had to carry a weapon when working. His uncle insisted on it.

It was agreed that in exchange for Sal's cooperation, twenty-four-hour security surveillance would be immediately placed on Sal and his family. Sal was to establish contact only through Bill, by asking for a meeting to be arranged, or by asking Bill to convey information to Mike. No one else would be involved since it was very dangerous for Sal to suddenly have new friends unknown to the family. As they heard the rest of the group noisily come in through the patio door, Mike hastily promised that Sal would be advised in advance of any raid. He also emphasized that it was the intent of all involved to keep the legitimate part of the company in operation, even though it might be at a reduced level of activity for awhile.

During the drive back to the Battista residence in Vancouver, everyone was enthused about the friendship and hospitality that they had received from Mike and Susan. They had experienced a beautiful day, wonderful food, great views and super people. What a way to spend a Sunday afternoon. Sal, in particular, seemed much more relaxed than he had been in many days. As he drove, he spoke positively of the future and their continuing friendship with the Hanleys. Even the thought of the Monday morning return to work didn't dampen his spirits at all.

Thirty-four

The dark blue Ford Explorer was sitting in space number seven with the front doors open and the engine running. Mr. Douglas Bowen, a Hertz Number One Gold Club customer and his business partner Mr. Donald McRae walked up and put their large briefcases in the back and then settled into the front seat. The two men were relaxed on this sunny Friday morning, having just arrived on the 9:30 a.m. WestJet flight from Edmonton. As they pulled out of the Vancouver International Airport parking lot and headed towards Highway 99 South, a beat up old pickup truck eased out of a parking space and began to follow them at a discrete distance.

Of course, the plainclothes constable driving the truck knew that the individuals he was tailing were really Dominic Salvatore and John Sabatini, who much earlier this morning had left Vancouver on the first Air Canada flight to Edmonton before making the return trip under one of their many assumed identities. For months now their weekly routine of flying out of town early on a Friday morning, returning to rent a car for travel to a secluded beach on Vancouver Island, then going through the process in reverse on Saturday afternoon was well known by now to the RCMP investigators assigned to the case. They even knew where each transfer of duffel bags packed full of drugs to a QHRS truck making its Saturday morning rounds took place. Similarly, they now knew the names and routes of all of the other senior company managers doing the same thing each weekend. They had more than enough evidence to bring down the whole drug operation, but one vital element in the plan was still missing, the necessary evidence to bring murder charges against Salvatore and Sabatini.

As the large Ford SUV moved off Highway 99 and on to Route 17 towards the Tsawwassen ferry terminal, the pick up truck continued south on 99 to ensure that the tail wasn't too obvious. The constable knew perfectly well that they were headed to the terminal and the vehicle description and license number had already been called in to an undercover constable working as a terminal agent and assigned to note the island destination of each of the vehicles of interest. As expected, the SUV moved from the ticket booth into the line for the 12:45 p.m. sailing to Duke Point near Nanaimo.

The next segment of the adventure got more interesting as the tail continued on Vancouver Island with a Nanaimo constable following the car north along the Island Highway. Every week the ultimate destination was different. A secluded cove on Denman Island or a deserted beach near Tofino, or occasionally just to an out of the way marina at Qualicum Beach. But not, so far, the location that Inspector Mike Hanley really wanted them to head for, the lonely beach on Quadra Island.

As the pair of unmarked cars which had alternately been maintaining the surveillance neared that vital junction of Highways Nineteen and Four where the target would either continue north or swing to the west towards Alberni, the alertness level was cranked up a bit. Unfortunately, a large slow truck had pulled out in front of the lead car which was holding back to avoid being seen just before the junction, and no one saw which way the Ford went. As a radio alert quickly went out, one car went up Four while the other continued on Nineteen and additional surveillance vehicles were called in. It was soon confirmed that the target was still headed north so, following standing orders, Inspector Hanley was informed. An hour later, when the vehicle passed through Courtenay still headed north, Mike Hanley alerted "E" Division Headquarters and put the Island District Criminal Investigation Section on standby.

✸ Thirty-five

Corporal Sarah Mathews hung up the phone after her conversation with Bill Patterson. She didn't like to call him at home, but this Friday it had been essential that she reach him right after he got home from work. Bill had immediately called Allison, who was surprised to hear from him so early on a Friday evening. He quickly explained that it was important that he talk to Sal privately away from their house and asked her to call Cheryl and invite her to go shopping with her that evening to pick out a prom dress. He mentioned that it was all about a confidential problem at work and that he would give her the details later.

Sal first dropped Allison, Cheryl and the baby off at the Metrotown Mall, and then he and Bill continued down Nelson Avenue and proceeded along Marine Drive. Sal looked in the rear view mirrors nervously, hoping to spot anyone who might be tailing them. He knew as soon as Cheryl had told him about Allison's request that something important was about to happen. What he didn't know or he would have been even more nervous, was that as soon as he had pulled away from his house to go and pick up Allison and Bill a car had pulled out of a parking spot further down his street and began to follow him. This event had even surprised the plainclothes constable sitting in his unmarked car who was just about to do the same thing. As the three vehicles continued down Victoria Drive four or five car lengths apart, the constable initiated an urgent radio conversation.

Passing Forty-second Street, the car following closely behind Sal was suddenly involved in a minor fender bender as a small truck pulled out of a side street without stopping. As a larger car driven by a man who seemed amused at the whole thing passed the scene, the aggrieved occupants of the damaged car jumped out to yell and threaten the truck driver with bodily harm. Apologizing profusely in somewhat broken English, the offending driver put up with the threats and verbal abuse until, having worked himself up to a fury with his inability to scare him, the automobile driver foolishly pulled out a gun. The truck driver then seemed transformed as he promptly used the best of spoken English and grammatically correct phrases to arrest them, put on the cuffs and read them their rights. He was sure that he could hold them for at least twenty-four hours for aggravated assault and threatening a peace officer before a lawyer could have them released.

Carefully following Bill's directions, Sal finally pulled into the parking lot behind the building at 657 West Thirty-seventh Avenue. They scurried up to the door where Corporal Sarah Mathews offered greetings and quickly guided them into a small conference room. After being introduced to Staff Sergeant Tom Guinness, who had been appointed the NCOIC of the raiding party, they sat at the table going over the QHRS warehouse building plans that Bill had drawn from memory. Sal marked in several corrections that the staff sergeant would incorporate by the next morning. They also carefully marked the locations of each of the inside and outside yard surveillance camera locations that Sal and Bill could remember and noted the number of monitors at the guard desk inside the entrance to the special orders department. Sal agreed to be at work a little early and be available near the inside entrance at the proper time. He was also made to promise that he would get out of the way and follow Bill into a safe place as soon as the team gained access to the secure areas.

Much later, carefully watching for anyone that might be following them, Sal and Bill returned to Metrotown to pick up Cheryl and Allison who had a very successful shopping trip and were restrained enough not to ask the boys about their evening adventures.

Thirty-six

The two businessmen finished their third cup of coffee after a superb dinner at Painter's Lodge in Campbell River. The bill was paid in cash with a generous tip added, and then they strolled leisurely to their car. Taking their time, they drove to the ferry terminal and got into the short line waiting for the 9:30 p.m. sailing to Quadra Island, totally oblivious to the frenzied activity that had been generated by their seemingly innocent activities.

As soon as their car had pulled into the lodge parking lot and it had become obvious that they were not traveling any further north on Vancouver Island that evening, orders were issued from Island District Headquarters at a rapid rate. Shortly after receiving an urgent dispatch call, the fast RCMP patrol vessel *Nadon* left Comox with a six-person special response team on board. The team was dressed in black and wore rubber boots with thick woolen socks pulled over them to muffle sound. At about the same time Corporal Ken Mullet had just completed a long telephone conversation with Inspector Hanley, and was walking down to the vessel at the ferry terminal wharf on Quadra Island to confer with his old friend, Gus Jenkins, who was on duty as evening shift captain.

Thirty minutes later as the ferry pulled into the Campbell

River Terminal, Gus told the mate that he would load the cars this trip and that the mate should take a break and just standby in the wheelhouse. After loading the waiting cars in record time and observing the occupants of each one very carefully, Gus had a seaman watch the ramp while he walked up to the pay phone on the wharf. Contacting the Quadra Island Detachment, Gus told Ken that there was absolutely no doubt that the two businessmen in the SUV were the same men that he saw leave the island last October. This meant that they were Dominic Salvatore and John Sabatini. Gus then casually strolled back on board, climbed the stairs to the wheelhouse, and proceeded to ease the ship out of the terminal.

Ken Mullett had Constable Ed Brewer park his cruiser in the usual observation spot at the Quadra Island Terminal parking lot while he raced up the Heriot Bay Road to meet the team arriving on the Nadon. He didn't want the normal Friday evening routine changed in any way during this return visit of his prime suspects. He wanted them to feel very secure in repeating their seemingly routine activities during this visit to his island jurisdiction. Rapidly making two trips from the *Nadon* to the secluded beach, Ken transported the team and their equipment to the area where they would begin the long late evening wait in concealment until, with any luck at all, their quarry would arrive for their lucrative beach party.

The last glimmering of light after sunset was reflected on the water at one end of Quathiaski Cove as the parking lot lights slowly came on in the terminal area. The ferry turned smartly around the point and headed directly for the slip as the passengers on board hastily returned to their automobiles. The two in the blue SUV hadn't budged during the trip, even though Gus had hoped that they would do something to permit him to at least yell at them for breaking some minor rule or another. *"Oh well,"* he thought, *"tomorrow morning would be a completely different story if the overnight activities occurred the way he thought they would."*

As the cars came off the ferry and passed his parking spot, Ed Brewer carefully avoided looking directly at THE vehicle as it passed him. He saw enough though that he would instantly recognize the two occupants when next he saw them. After the SUV had passed from the parking area and turned onto the road, Ed noted that a beat-up old jeep with a young man behind the wheel began following two or three car lengths behind it. Ed then started his cruiser and slowly performed a routine patrol of the village area to make sure that the suspects hadn't looped back and parked nearby. He then returned to the detachment office.

"Shit," said Corporal Mullet as he loudly put down the phone as Ed entered the office. Responding to Ed's quizzical look, he continued, "I thought the son-of-a-bitch was a friend of mine. You can't trust commissioned officers in this outfit."

"You want to tell me what your problem is boss?" Ed asked.

"Inspector Michael Edward Hanley, RCMP, is the problem. The *SOB* says that I am to stay here in the detachment office as the scene coordinator and that I'm not to go to the beach area. He says that I'm too emotionally involved in the outcome of this case. Bullshit, I say."

"Well, I hate to agree with him, but this time I have to, you are," Ed replied.

Just then, three clicks came from the radio as a microphone was keyed on and off, which meant that Constable Cairns had seen the blue SUV turn down Bold Point Road as he continued past the intersection in his jeep. Hearing that, Ed Brewer quickly moved outside to his cruiser and proceeded up the road towards the junction to block the exit from the Bold Point area and prevent any traffic movement in or out until morning.

Hearing the same signal, Corporal Kenyon concealed his

team in the brush at the edge of the beach, two on each side of the access lane, and two across the road from the lane entrance. With black clothing and blackened faces, they sat virtually motionless in the bush patiently waiting for the order to move in while they watched the SUV back down the lane to the beach.

Thirty-seven

aptain Oley squinted as he checked his position on the radar and then scanned the channel for the buoy marking the entrance to Upper Heriot Bay. The radar had not picked up the *Nadon*, which was drifting without lights in the shadow of Read Island, but *Nadon*'s radar clearly displayed the *Glory Bee*. As the fishing vessel slowly continued parallel to the shoreline, Oley's two sons opened the hatch and began raking aside the ice that had concealed the four duffel bags in the fish hold. Slowing to bare steerageway, Captain Oley carefully watched the beach area with his binoculars until he saw a single quick flash from a light ashore. He then let the vessel drift as he hurried out of the wheelhouse to help lower the skiff and load the heavy duffel bags into the boat.

Meanwhile, at Quathiaski Cove, the ferry eased into the Quadra Island Terminal after completing the last trip of the night at 11:40 p.m. The seamen doubled up on the mooring lines after the last car had driven off, then prepared to guide the fuel truck on-board as it backed down the ramp. Meanwhile, Chief Engineer Jill Norman having secured the main engines sent Oiler Jake McAllen up the ladder to the vehicle deck to connect the shore power cable and start filling the fresh water tanks. She then carefully sounded the fuel storage tanks in preparation for refueling. Completing that job she went to the main switchboard and saw that the shore power available indicator light was on. She quickly paralleled the generator with shore power, tripped the breaker and shut down the diesel. The silence was blissful, just the gentle whirring of the vent fans and the sound of a couple of pumps in operation.

Meanwhile, Captain Gus along with the mate and the two seamen secured the wheelhouse and accommodation areas and went ashore, slowly walking up to their cars in the crew parking area. Jill stood at the fuel oil filling manifold, intently watching the tank level indicators and operating the filling valves as fuel from the tank truck was gravity fed into the storage tanks. The sound powered telephone rang twice as the signal that the tank truck was empty and the valves could be secured. Jill verified the level indicator values one last time and then went up to the deck to sign the receipt for the fuel and make sure that the water tanks were full. She and Jake then did a final check of the machinery spaces, ensuring that everything was secure for the night. Jake went ashore while Jill first completed the engine room log entries and then went up to the engineer's cabin to complete the fueling records. After that, she wearily changed and left the ship, following the usual end of shift routine.

Just after driving out of the parking lot, Jill's usual routine changed drastically. Instead of driving straight home as she normally did, she went to the Whisky Point Resort parking lot. She parked the car near the restaurant entrance and then quickly got into the back of a windowless van where she met Captain Gus, Jake, an RCMP constable and a driver. The driver introduced himself as Staff Sergeant John Blake as he backed out of the parking space and proceeded to the ferry terminal. Driving down through the parking lot to the loading ramp, he turned off the headlights then quickly turned and backed down towards the ferry. Stopping just short of the end, he paused as the mate jumped out and quickly lowered the apron onto the deck then motioned the driver to continue. After the van was parked in the center of the vehicle deck, everyone got out and scattered to different parts of the ship while the mate raised the apron once again.

Jill started the still warm diesel generator set, put it on line and tripped the shore power breaker. Then she proceeded to open all of the circuit breakers feeding the normal lighting panels outside of the machinery spaces which left only a few emergency lighting fixtures in operation elsewhere. Jake disconnected the shore power cable and then went up to the emergency generator room where he opened the circuit breakers feeding the emergency lighting panels. This left most of the ship in total darkness. Jill then started the main engines and transferred control to the wheelhouse console.

After hearing a short, gentle ring on the bow sound-powered telephone, the mate let go the mooring lines and Gus slowly backed the vessel out of the slip in the dark then turned and proceeded down the strait and around Cape Mudge. Carefully watching the radar screen, Gus quietly gave helm orders to the mate as they slowly moved towards Marina Island where he stopped in the shadows near the shore and drifted. This action immediately violated several Coast Guard Regulations, including the International Rules of the Road since he had also turned off the navigation lights. While Gus continued to watch the radar display, the mate and Staff Sergeant Blake continuously scanned the channel using their binoculars. Jake walked carefully around the outside decks, making sure that no light was escaping from inside the vessel.

✲ Thirty-eight

The skiff was nearly awash with the total weight of the duffel bags and two husky fishermen as they approached the shoreline. Another brief flash from the light ashore directed them to a landing and the man in the bow prepared to jump ashore with a line as his companion worked the oars as hard as he could to give momentum as they hit the beach. Upon landing they were met by two men who hastily began to assist in dragging the duffel bags to the open rear hatch of the SUV where they were loaded.

Just as the fourth bag arrived at the rear and the first was being picked up with much grunting and swearing for loading into the SUV, the men were blinded as six high-powered spot lights illuminated the scene from either side of the beach.

"Corporal Kenyon, Royal Canadian Mounted Police," came a booming voice from beyond the lights, "Drop to the sand, spread your arms and legs, and freeze."

Three of the four men did exactly that. The fourth hastily drew a handgun from his pocket and quickly fired a series of shots directly at the offending spotlights. The crack of a rifle rang out and the shooter screamed as a bullet tore through his shoulder and knocked him to the sand. Taking advantage of the illumination from the spotlights which had been mounted on poles driven into the sand some distance away from the lane area during the night, Corporal Kenyon's team quickly moved in and cuffed the astounded individuals lying on the beach. Dominic Salvatore, who was in shock from the massive wound in his shoulder, had one wrist cuffed to his belt at the back of his trousers while a pad was applied to his wound to slow the bleeding. No one really wanted him to die on the beach when there was such a good possibility of having him convicted and jailed for life instead.

The moment that the shots were fired on the beach, Captain Oley jammed the *Glory Bee's* throttle full ahead and proceeded down the channel without a thought of what might happen to his two sons. He was intent on getting away to Powell River and to the confidential location where the remainder of his payment for this voyage would be waiting. As soon as the fishing vessel's movement became obvious on the radar display, the NCOIC of *Nadon* also pushed his throttles to the full ahead position and began pursuit.

After hearing two clicks of a microphone being keyed on the VHF radio, Gus gently eased the ferry's propulsion control lever to the full ahead position and began moving the darkened ship towards the center of the channel. As Capt. Oley gradually became aware of the fast moving vessel which had appeared some distance behind him and was closing fairly quickly, he nervously began thinking about shortcuts to the main southbound shipping channel where he could blend in with other traffic. Suddenly, he was blinded by the beam of a twelve-inch searchlight, which was directly ahead and aimed right into his wheelhouse window. Panicking, he hastily pulled the throttle to the full astern position and turned the wheel hard over to starboard. He fetched up suddenly, bouncing the *Glory Bee* against the rubbing rail of a seemingly huge vessel, which had loomed up out of the darkness when he had turned away from the glare of the searchlight. As he came to a stop alongside, lights suddenly appeared throughout the ship and it became apparent that he had somehow encountered a BC Ferry traveling through the inky darkness. Captain Oley was about to turn the wheel and push his throttle full ahead once again to try to get away from the side of the ferry when he saw Staff Sergeant Blake jump onto the foredeck and take careful aim at his head with his service revolver. He looked around wildly, and saw a constable on the vehicle deck of the ferry aim a rifle at him through the wheelhouse door at the same time as *Nadon* arrived to further illuminate the scene with a searchlight. Captain Oley put his hands up and surrendered without a word being spoken.

Meanwhile on the beach, Corporal Kenyon made sure that the three relatively healthy suspects were handcuffed and shackled, then checked on the condition of Salvatore before reaching for his radio. "Quadra Special Team, Courtenay"

"Courtenay, Quadra Team" came the response, "read you faintly but clearly."

"Quadra Team, Courtenay: The turkeys are in the pen, one with a badly broken wing. We require an ambulance stat and all Quadra units for immediate transportation to Heriot Bay."

"Courtenay, Quadra Team, 10-4. Will request Quadra 1 support immediately."

Changing frequencies, Kenyon called again "Quadra Special Team, *Nadon*"

"*Nadon*, Quadra Team," came the booming voice of Sergeant Miller of the *Nadon*, "what else can we do for you today?"

"Need immediate rendezvous at the Heriot Bay Ferry Terminal for team and suspect transport and a high speed run to Campbell River. One suspect is badly wounded and needs hospitalization. Quadra 1 has been dispatched for ground transportation and an ambulance has been called."

"10-4, we still have a couple of things to do here and then we're on the way."

The *Nadon* took the handcuffed Captain Oley, Staff Sergeant Blake and the constable on board. Then the second-in-command transferred to *Glory Bee* with orders to take her into Campbell River so that the mobile crime lab could do a thorough inspection to see just what kind of cargo had been stowed in the fish hold. *Nadon* then got underway with a final wave to Gus and the others on the ferry and headed off at twenty-eight knots for Heriot Bay.

Ken Mullet was in a much happier frame of mind as he raced down Bold Point Road towards the beach area. He had just been on the phone with Inspector Hanley before leaving the detachment office and received the order to detain the healthy suspects on Quadra Island so that there would be no chance that word of their arrest would leak out before Saturday night. Salvatore would still be transported to the Campbell River Hospital, but his condition would be evaluated and determined to be far too serious to permit use of a telephone much before Sunday. Inspector Hanley would personally visit all concerned in the morning.

Thirty-nine

Bill Patterson was tired . . .dog tired. Drag-ass weary, as he trudged from the bus stop and across the parking lot to the building's employee entrance. It wasn't as though this was anything new. It was a normal part of his weekend routine to report by 5:00 a.m. to begin the morning delivery run. But it had been a long Friday evening by the time the meeting at headquarters was over. They had collected Allison and Cheryl at the Metrotown Mall and taken everyone home. Even the thought of the trip to Nanaimo this morning with the scenic ferry crossing and a free lunch didn't cheer him up much, because he knew that this was going to be a very long day. The longest of his career so far and the culmination of his undercover assignment, if all went as planned.

Bill stirred himself though and greeted Chuck with the usual degree of enthusiasm as they quickly checked the cargo manifests, then boarded the truck and began the trip to the ferry terminal. The trip across the Strait of Georgia was as pleasant as ever, as was the breakfast break in the cafeteria, and before he knew it they were proceeding down the ramp at the Departure Bay Terminal ready to begin their busy morning delivery rounds.

At about the same time, a blue SUV, in response to the signal from the seaman on deck, proceeded down the ramp to board the small ferry loading up for the first morning trip to Campbell River. The two well-dressed businessmen in the car looked straight ahead as they drove along the deck and stopped just short of the barrier at the forward end of the vehicle deck. The mate on duty noted that the car must have a heavy load in the rear, since the back end was much lower than would be normal for a tourist returning home from the island with just luggage and souvenirs. The mate also remembered the questions that had been raised last fall when a similar vehicle had visited the island, and made a mental note to tell Ken Mullett about the vehicle later in the day.

As the SUV headed south on Highway Nineteen towards Nanaimo, the driver set the cruise control at exactly the speed limit, since the last thing the businessmen wanted was a series of embarrassing questions from a highway patrol constable who would insist on viewing driver's licenses, insurance and registration forms. And so they continued south, with annoyed stares and the occasional finger presented to them as speeding cars rushed past them eager to get on with their busy Saturday schedule. They did jot down the license numbers of the rudest offenders though, just in case some opportunity for vengeance should present itself in the near future.

The blue Explorer finally arrived in Nanaimo and pulled into the Bastion Inn parking lot. Carefully looking around as they slowly drove towards the QHRS truck in the lot and seeing nothing suspicious, they parked with the rear of the vehicle lined up with the side door on the truck. Moving quickly, one man found the right key and opened the truck door while his partner opened the SUV hatch. Then, working together, they lifted one heavy duffel bag at a time up from the back of the SUV and heaved it into the dark interior of the refrigerated truck. Quickly securing the hatch and the truck door, they hastily drove out of the parking lot and headed down the road towards the ferry terminal. They hadn't noticed the figure crouched on the roof of the inn with a portable radio in his hand.

Following the usual Saturday in Nanaimo routine, Chuck and Bill left the restaurant men's room and strolled over to the truck to begin the trip home. Just as Chuck was unlocking the cab door, an RCMP cruiser appeared from nowhere and pulled up beside him. Another unit simultaneously pulled up on the opposite side, nearly pinning Bill against the truck door. Next thing they both knew, they were on the ground spread-eagled, handcuffed and being roughly searched for weapons. Bill broke out into a sweat as he visualized the major plans for the day being destroyed due to overeager local constables trying to prove some sort of point. He started to protest his treatment and was kneed in the back for his trouble and told to shut up.

Pulled to his feet and told to unlock the cab, Chuck was white with fear as a sniffer dog on a leash was brought over to the truck by one of the constables. As soon as the cab was open, the dog leaped inside and barked in frenzy as he tried to claw through the rear seat back. Chuck was told in no uncertain terms to release the latch. Then, when the safe door was exposed, he had no option but to follow the order to open it. The dog barked wildly as he sniffed the bags of money revealed on the inside ledge as Chuck was deposited none to gently into the rear seat of the cruiser. Bill was promptly thrown in beside him, still trying to protest his innocence. They watched in anguish as the truck was thoroughly searched, but from their position in the back seat of the cruiser they didn't see that the duffel bags were superficially inspected then left alone.

They were transported to the local police station. Chuck was really in a state of torment as he realized that he was about to lose his highly paid job, his home life, and his freedom. He also realized that the very future of the company was at stake and vehemently demanded his right to make a phone call. After being sarcastically reminded that he had obviously been watching too much TV and getting the wrong idea about prisoner's rights, he continued to loudly protest as he was booked and then roughly propelled down the hall and into a cell.

Bill tried in vain to get someone to pay attention to his whispered, urgent request to speak to a supervisor or make an official telephone call as he was being processed for booking. His pleas were also ignored as he was being pushed down the hall and into the cell next to Chuck, where he knew he had to stay quiet.

Forty

Wilma Parker was enjoying the beginning of her early morning shift in one of the many Tsawwassen Terminal fare collection booths. She had just met a group of really nice young men and women in a white fifteen-passenger van that drove up to her and bought return tickets to Vancouver Island. It was one of several identical vans in her line, which were loaded with equally cheery young adults who were obviously on their way to some sort of church-sponsored outing on the island. The rear section behind the seats in each van was loaded with luggage, so they must have planned to be away for at least a long weekend. Strangely enough, though, they were not all going to the same destination. At least not initially, since some bought tickets for Swartz Bay, others for Nanaimo and a couple for the direct trip to the Gulf Islands. They seemed to know each other pretty well though, because they all got out of the vans to chat and kid around while waiting in the boarding lanes.

The blue SUV had made good time coming through town from the hotel parking lot. It turned into the driveway and went behind the Nanaimo detachment building and into a parking place where it couldn't be seen from the street. The two businessmen emerged, stretched while looking around and then hastily removed their suit coats, ties and the rubber gloves that they were wearing. Constables Brewer and Cairns then scurried into the building through the side door and headed for the sergeant's office to drop the car keys on her desk and ask for transportation back to Campbell River.

A half-hour later, a constable came down the hall from the office and yelled out,

"All right lovebirds, which one of you is going to sing first?" from just outside the cell doors as he glared at Chuck and Bill in turn.

"What about you, Patterson? Want to come and tell the sergeant a nice story?" Unlocking the cell door, he reached in and grabbed Bill by the back of his shirt collar, pulled him from the cell then pushed him up the corridor as he called out, "See you soon Rossi, don't worry too much about Patterson. You might see him again some day."

As soon as the door from the cellblock corridor to the office area was closed and locked behind them, the burly constable let go of Bill's shirt, apologized, stuck out his hand and said, "Welcome to Nanaimo, Constable Patterson. The duty sergeant really is ready to hear your story." Bill was then ushered into the inner office where he met Sergeant Hathaway, who had just arranged for the highway patrol to take Brewer and Cairns home.

Bill was requested to explain the details of the truck's regular morning schedule while in Nanaimo and identify each of the stops that were made as Chuck delivered his special orders. Bill provided that much information but explained that if additional details were required, Inspector Hanley must be contacted first, since an undercover operation was still in progress. The sergeant agreed, acknowledging that this was just a small piece of the action, then arranged to have Bill driven back to the truck in an unmarked car so that he could move on to the Departure Bay Terminal and catch the next ferry back to Horseshoe Bay and Vancouver.

As the ferry from Tsawwassen was approaching the Duke Point Terminal, a group of young adults made their way between the rows of cars on the vehicle deck to their white van. With some good-natured shoving and jostling, they climbed in and prepared to disembark. Everyone was feeling satisfied after a prolonged visit to the breakfast buffet and was now ready for some serious recreation and exercise. Unfortunately, no one would get any for quite some time. The ferry nudged the pier, was secured, and the vehicles slowly began to drive off the ship and through the terminal area to the exit. The white van didn't follow this normal routine; however, but was suddenly directed to the front of the line so that it could race up the highway and through town to the Departure Bay Terminal to immediately enter the line of traffic waiting to board the next ferry to Horseshoe Bay and the mainland.

Meanwhile, Bill eased his large truck into the lane for the ferry terminal tollbooth still feeling shaken by his arrest and the short period of jail time. This experience was not part of any plan that he had been aware of, and he had been sure that his participation for the rest of the day had been compromised. But maybe not. After all, he did have possession of the truck and the cargo in the back was still there as far as he knew. So maybe things were on track and Chuck's early removal from the scene had been planned. He approached the booth, paid his fare and moved into the assigned lane to await boarding. He would have to be extra careful because he was not used to driving the truck through the narrow traffic lanes onto the ship. He noticed two other QHRS trucks waiting in the lanes ahead and hoped that he wouldn't have to explain Chuck's absence to the other drivers. If they went straight up to the lounge area after boarding, they might not notice that Bill was alone.

Moving aboard the ship with considerable caution as he followed the seaman's directions, Bill parked in his designated lane and waited in the cab until the lanes around him were full and the cars were secured. After hearing the ship's engines accelerate and feeling the motion of the ship getting underway, he climbed out of the cab and immediately noticed the white van that was parked directly behind him and the man who was approaching him wearing the gray shirt of a QHRS driver's helper. Carefully looking around before shaking hands and handing Bill a blue driver's shirt, he then went on to unlock and slide open the side loading door of the truck. As soon as that was done, all of the van's occupants except the driver hastily climbed out of the van, ran down the side of the truck and climbed in through the open door, after quickly heaving their equipment bags in first. The first man then slid the door shut and carefully locked it.

Further up the vehicle deck, a similar scenario was taking place, with the occupants of two other white vans climbing into QHRS truck cargo compartments and also taking over the cabs. In these vans, both the driver and an assistant remained in the vehicle. As the ferry approached the terminal, four well fed QHRS drivers and helpers who were threading their way between vehicles to reach their trucks were astounded to find their cabs already occupied. Finding the truck doors locked with the imposters inside wearing the correct QHRS uniforms and grinning at them, they began banging on the truck doors and demanding to be let in.

At this point they were grabbed from behind, wrestled to the deck, handcuffed and deposited none too gently into the vans parked behind their trucks. All they could do was swear and threaten as they watched their trucks being driven off the ferry and through the terminal to the highway without them. Similar fun and games were taking place on all the ferries approaching the Greater Vancouver area terminals that had QHRS trucks on board.

Forty-one

Sal was nervous and the more he tried to suppress it the more concerned he became. He had started his shift at the usual time and had checked and double checked that the personnel inside the special orders department were ready to follow the normal routine. Since Saturday was the busiest evening of the week with all of the new supplies coming in to be processed into retail delivery packages, a full crew was on. They were anxiously awaiting the arrival of the first truck so that they could get started, since everyone was hoping to get home on time.

For some reason, the trucks were very late. Even the short-haul ones from Powell River and Sechelt had not arrived yet. With fourteen truckloads to process during the shift, everyone would really have to hump to get finished on time. Joe DeSilva, who was working special orders today, had noticed Sal's jumpiness and made a mental note to tell John Sabatini about it when he got in later this evening.

As Bill rolled along the Upper Levels Highway, his newly arrived helper was busy on his portable radio trying to coordinate the schedules of the other trucks which had just left their respective ferry terminals. The two that had been ahead of Bill moving out of the terminal had slowed to a crawl on the highway until Bill passed them. Then they dutifully took their place in the line behind him as others progressively joined in.

Staff Sergeant Tom Guinness had set up his command post two blocks from the warehouse and was directing the movements of his team into their positions around the complex. While the QHRS trucks were slowly moving along the highways from both north and south of the city to converge onto Commercial Drive, the movements to completely surround the warehouse, both inside and outside the perimeter fence, had been completed. Initially, sharpshooters had taken out key surveillance cameras, then the backup teams consisting of RCMP members from detachments all over the Greater Vancouver area, supplemented by Vancouver City Police Department personnel, moved into their prearranged positions and concealed themselves as much as possible.

"Sal," Cliff Roper called out testily from the lobby guard desk while easing his gun out of its holster, "two more cameras have just gone haywire, both the one by the main gate and the one looking down at the unloading docks. That's four screens that have gone blank in the last hour. You better get one of those maintenance weenies in from home real fast to get us back on line or your uncle will throw a shit fit when he gets in tonight."

Sal said that he would go out to the electrical equipment room in the general warehouse area to see if he could see anything obviously wrong, then call maintenance from the warehouse foreman's desk while he was at it. He perfunctorily looked around the room and thought about how long he should be away from the lobby and had an idea. Quickly checking the various distribution panel directory cards, he found what he was looking for and opened the circuit breaker labeled security door circuits. He then returned to the special orders lobby access door and operated the cipher lock to open it. Nothing happened, he pounded on the door so that Cliff would let him in. Cliff yelled through the door, demanding to know who it was and Sal replied just as loudly that now even the fucking door lock wasn't working properly.

Just as he was swinging the heavy steel door open to let Sal in, the phone rang at the guard desk. Cliff picked it up, listened, and then announced over the internal PA system that the first two trucks had finally rolled in through the front gates. This resulted in a flurry of activity as the four-man unloading teams, wearing the required black shirts, assembled in the lobby ready to run out to the trucks and drag in the cargo bags. At this point Cliff noticed that the camera monitoring the lobby door was out of action along with all the electric locks.

⎈ Forty-two

Bill climbed down from his truck and moved towards the driver's lounge, making sure that the other drivers who had just backed their trucks into the unloading bays followed him. The driver's helpers moved off towards the employee lunchroom as usual, then quickly made their moves to arrest and handcuff any warehouse employees that were out on the floor, pushing them into the lunchroom with them. The innocent and the guilty could be sorted out later when the building was secured. When Bill was sure that they were all out of sight, he pushed the button outside the lounge door to ring the bell in the special orders lobby to signal that the trucks were ready for unloading and that the driving teams had moved away from the area. As Sal held the door open and Cliff stood there with his weapon drawn, the black shirted group immediately jogged out to the truck bays with the four person crews peeling off progressively to approach the side cargo door of each truck.

The first team unlocked and slid open the side door of Bill's truck, automatically reaching in and switching on the cargo bay light. Nothing happened, so the first two men just reached in to grab the straps on the heavy duffel bags that were normally just inside the door. There was nothing there which was strange since they were far too heavy for anyone loading them into the truck to move them much further into the interior. Swearing, since it was too dark to see much, all four of them stumbled into the cargo compartment to see where the bags were. They never found out. Each man was swiftly and silently knocked to the floor, cuffed to a cargo tie-down rail and had a piece of duct tape slapped over his mouth. Then the replacement team of black shirted unloaders dragged the duffel bags out of the truck and proceeded with them towards the special orders lobby.

The initial team quickly approached the lobby door, dragging the heavy bags behind them. They paused while three other teams caught up with them and then banged on the door while shouting for someone to open it. As Sal swung the door open, they quickly pushed past him with their heads down and headed for the second door and into the lab. Before Cliff could react, one of the team members knocked the gun from his hand and subdued him while Bill led the first contingent of well-armed "drivers" and "helpers" through the lobby and into the plant. Others quickly followed carrying portable fire extinguishers. Sal had told the planning team that one of the lab contingency plans in case of a raid was to set as much on fire as possible to destroy evidence and to create a diversion to cover an escape through the rear doors.

Many shots rang out in the back rooms of the laboratory complex where the teams had dropped the duffel bags and begun subduing and arresting everyone within reach. Sal was whisked out of the lobby area and escorted to the driver's lounge where a forward command post had recently been set up. The inner perimeter team had been moved up to surround the building complex and the outer team had been moved inside the grounds. Many patrol vehicles were now parked inside the fenced area with lights still flashing, as the police reinforcements rushed into the warehouse. Similarly, Bill was grabbed and manhandled out of harm's way. His court testimony would be far too valuable in the future to risk having him accidentally injured now.

There was ferocious fighting in the now smoky lab complex as the desperate workers first put up serious resistance to the assault, then frantically tried to escape through the rear doors and the tunnel to the maintenance building. A few overwhelmed constables called for more reinforcements, who were rushed in as the designated fire fighters called for more extinguishers. The police personnel outside the building were now fully occupied rounding up those who had escaped from the lab and hustled them into buses which had been brought in as temporary holding centers and prisoner transport vehicles.

Far above the lab and warehouse areas in the third floor executive suites, the elderly Guido Battista, the Chairman of the Board of QHRS and the revered patriarch of the companies' founding families, was gradually becoming aware that something was not quite right in the plant. He heard a lot of unusual noise in the distance and was sure that he had heard the sounds of shots being fired. Concerned, he picked up the phone and dialed the extension for the guard desk in the special orders lobby. When he got no reply from a position which was to be manned twenty-four hours a day, he began to really worry and called out to his personal assistant and bodyguard, ordering him to take the private elevator down to the lab to see what was happening.

When the elevator door opened in the lobby, a sight that he had thought he would never see greeted him. Uniformed RCMP constables were seated at the guard desk, maintaining surveillance at the complex door, which was wedged wide open. In a panic, he drew his weapon and hastily fired. The shot, missing everyone in the room, bounced off of the steel door and went out into the warehouse to wedge itself into a pillar. He was promptly shot in the arm for his trouble as one of the constables wheeled around and spotted him in the open doorway of the elevator. The door hadn't been noticed previously, since the sliding veneer panel which served as the outer elevator door had completely concealed the entrance.

Two constables quickly dragged him out of the way as two others got into the elevator and pushed the "up" button. Crouched with their weapons drawn as the elevator came to a stop and the doors slowly opened, they leaped into the corridor with each one covering a different direction down the hall. There was no one in sight. They were startled as Guido called out, demanding to know what had been seen downstairs. Moving towards his voice, they managed to hold fire as he came out of his office to berate his aide for not immediately answering him. He crumpled to the floor in shock as he realized that the constables confronting him meant that his highly profitable family business enterprise was finished.

As the rounding up of evidence in the lab was taking place, which included fifty-six duffel bags stuffed with drugs and uncounted tens of thousands of dollars in cash, a thorough room by room search of the entire complex was taking place. Detective Sergeant Alex Stuart was standing in the middle of the warehouse floor watching the last of the suspects being led out to the buses when he was suddenly very startled and grabbed Staff Sergeant Guinness by the arm.

"Look," he shouted as he pointed, "that man in the blue shirt is one of them. He works here as a part time driver's helper."

"*That man* just happens to be Constable Bill Patterson," replied Guinness, "he's the undercover agent who made this whole raid possible."

"Constable Bill Patterson? You're crazy. He's just a high school kid!"

"That's what we wanted everyone to think," said Guinness raising his voice. "Patterson!" "Yes, staff sergeant," Bill replied crisply.

"Come over here please, I want you to meet someone."

"Yes, staff sergeant," Bill answered again as he marched over to the two men.

Grinning, he held out his hand to Detective Sergeant Stuart and thanked him for his assistance in making the raid possible. Stuart grumpily acknowledged Bill and then demanded to know if Allison was aware of any of this.

"No," Bill assured him and then asked that he be allowed to tell Allison about it himself after church tomorrow. They had plans to go out for brunch anyway, so it would be a good time to bring her up to speed.

Bill then requested that he and Sal be allowed to leave to get some sleep, since they both would have to be back early Sunday afternoon to supervise the loading crews getting the trucks ready for the regular Monday morning deliveries. Staff Sergeant Guinness gave his permission, so Bill found Sal and they slowly headed out to the parking lot where the excitement of rounding up and transporting prisoners was just about over. Bill readily accepted Sal's offer for a lift home and they agreed to meet at the warehouse office at 3:00 p.m. the next day.

When he got home, Bill, despite his fatigue, felt obliged to tell John and Anne Cassidy all about the raid and, in confidence, what the company was suspected of. John was not too surprised since he had noted that the pleasant, cooperative attitude of the drivers had changed over the last few years. John was very relieved when Bill told him that the legal side of the business would continue to operate under government oversight. John reiterated what Bill already knew that the hospitality industry could not tolerate the loss of their principal supplier. Bill finished the last of the tea and scone treat that Anne had provided and then wearily went off to bed.

⚙ Forty-three

The bright June morning sun was shining at the beginning of another beautiful Vancouver day as Bill pulled up in front of the Stuart residence. He had borrowed his aunt's car, and it was a real treat to be able to take Allison out by automobile for a change instead of by bus. In fact, it occurred to Bill that he could buy a car of his own now that the undercover part of his job was just about over. He walked quickly up the front steps and rang the doorbell, feeling somewhat conspicuous wearing a suit and tie instead of the usual jeans and sweatshirt.

The door swung open and Alex Stuart greeted Bill enthusiastically while ushering him into the living room, inviting him to sit down and chat while waiting for Allison. Mrs. Stuart was pleasantly surprised and pleased at her husband's friendly attitude, since she really liked Bill and thought that he was a good friend for Allison to have. In fact, Bill was engaged in an interesting conversation about police work with her father when Allison came into the room, looking radiant in a new spring outfit. Bill stood up to greet her and then they said quick "good-byes' to Allison's parents and headed out to the car. As soon as the door closed behind them, Alex hurried his wife into the kitchen, poured two cups of coffee, and proceeded to tell her all about Bill's real identity and job description.

Allison and Bill arrived at the front door of the church just as the liturgy was beginning, since Bill had no idea that parking places were so hard to find. That was totally outside of his small town experience and certainly was not a factor in regular bus travel to and from the church. They managed to find seats near the front on a side aisle just as the procession began and Bill was captivated once again by Allison's voice as she joined in singing the entrance hymn. When the mass was over and after participating in a very frustrating experience getting out of the parking lot in one piece, Bill first drove south to Marine Drive, then headed west for a leisurely trip through the University of British Columbia Campus. They continued on to Fourth Avenue and then down to the Kitsilano District, where he found a water view restaurant that was serving Sunday brunch.

After a surprisingly short wait, they were seated at a window table where a server soon approached with a Champaign bottle in her hand. After looking at them carefully, she decided not to fill their wine glasses and casually mentioned that various kinds of juices were available on the buffet whenever they were ready to help themselves. They lingered at their table for awhile, enjoying the view across English Bay and watching the freighters leisurely swinging around on their anchor chains as the wind slowly changed direction. Bill was agonizing over the timing of revealing his true story to Allison, should he wait until they had eaten, or begin right away? He wisely decided that it would be best during the desert and coffee phase when they were more relaxed; and at the appointed time, he swallowed hard and began to talk.

Bill began by telling Allison that he had something to tell her that didn't change their relationship in any way, other than the fact that he was a year older than she thought he was, and that he didn't have to choose a career after high school because he already had a steady job. He then went on to tell her what he had really done since leaving home in Alberta. Nothing was different in his life's story other than the previously unrevealed period of training in Regina at the RCMP Depot Division, undercover operative training and then arriving at the high school as a new student as part of his first undercover assignment.

Allison, who had been gazing contentedly at the anchored ships, turned towards him in amazement when he began to talk. She quickly realized what he had revealed and that just about everything she knew about him was true except for the one-year gap in his history. The fact that he had already graduated from high school and was going through the process for the second time seemed to surprise her far more than the account of his graduation from Depot Division and the reality of his identity as a police constable. At first, she had great difficulty in believing that he had not deliberately tried to deceive her as part of his undercover identity, but finally came to realize that they had indeed become good friends after his arrival at the school while he was beginning his normal activities. He couldn't possibly have known about her beforehand, somehow deciding to involve her in his undercover mission.

She sat silently for a long time after he had finished his story and continued to profess that his love for her was genuine and not a part of any covert activities. In fact, he reiterated how relieved he was to be able to finally tell her everything and truly hoped that she would be a confidant and a supporter during the final days of the case. He also told her how pleased he was that he now had her father's acceptance, which should make their continuing relationship a whole lot easier. He ended with a pledge to love her forever and begged her to consider him a vital part of her future plans after graduation.

Allison began to question him about the details of his job and what risks he and Sal might be exposed to while wrapping up the case. She had learned enough about the dangers of undercover work from her father to realize that it might not be as safe as Bill was trying to make it out to be. He assured her that he and the other team members were taking no chances and he was being particularly careful to make sure that she wouldn't be in any danger. After much discussion and many questions, some repeated three and four times, Allison finally became comfortable with what she had been told and became more accepting of Bill's new identity. She actually began to be proud of the fact that, as a new constable, he had been given a great deal of responsibility that normally would have been restricted to someone with a lot more experience.

Naturally, she now wanted to know what came next. Would he be able to stay in Vancouver or would he have to go somewhere back east?

Bill explained that since his undercover assignment was coming to an end, he would have to do a six-month tour of on-the-job field training in a busy detachment to learn what regular police work is all about in a large urban area. Fortunately, since the trial phase of the current operation was still to come and he would be needed as a witness, he could expect to stay around the Vancouver area for a long time. He thought that he would be assigned to the Burnaby, North Vancouver or perhaps the Surrey Detachments so that he was readily available for court testimony.

Allison expressed relief that this would fit in with her own plans to go to college locally, someplace like Simon Fraser University where she could save money by still living at home. Bill indicated that when this training thing was over and he became a full regular member of the force, they should seriously consider plans for marriage and a home of their own. As they were holding hands and contemplating that great idea, the server broke into their dreams by presenting the check.

Bill opened the passenger side door for Allison, waited until she was comfortably seated, then closed the door and went around to the driver's side. He started the engine, put the shift lever into reverse and glanced in the rear view mirror as he began to move. He then slammed his foot on the brake pedal and stopped six inches short of the side door of a Vancouver City Police Cruiser that had parked directly behind him. Just as he was saying, "What kind of a dumb maneuver is that guy trying to pull off?" there was a tapping on the driver's side window. Bill rolled down the window prepared to let loose on the city constable that stood, grinning, in front of him.

"Constable Patterson, I presume?"

"Yes, and what's it to you," Bill replied, clearly annoyed. "And furthermore, how in hell did you know who I am and where I was?"

"The Vancouver City Police also has ways of finding their man," retorted the officer with a chuckle. "But seriously, all units were given the car license plate number and told to find you immediately and pass the message that Inspector Hanley needs you at the QHRS facility right now. I have been ordered to take Miss Stuart home so that you can get there as quickly as possible."

Bill was more than a little dismayed to see his long anticipated Sunday afternoon with Allison evaporating into nothing and was very concerned that she would rapidly see the downside of being associated with an RCMP member. Allison was more than understanding; however, and as they got out of the car she reminded him of how often her mother and she had to change their weekend plans when her father was suddenly called into the station to handle some sort of emergency.

Giving the surprised Bill a quick kiss, Allison jumped into the front seat of the cruiser and as she was closing the car door, told him to phone her later. Bill watched them drive off, then got back into his aunt's car and broke the speed limit a few times rushing to find out what was now going on at work.

⚓ Forty-four

Bill drove into the QHRS compound, parked near a side door and ran inside to the special orders department to see what was happening. He was astounded to see Inspector Hanley, Sal, and several others standing at paper cutting machines scattered around the room rapidly trimming white bond paper into sizes resembling dollar bills.

"Grab a machine and start trimming," ordered the inspector.

"Yes sir," Bill replied, "but can I ask why and why now?"

"Do you see those empty duffel bags on the counter over there?" Hanley replied, then without waiting for an answer, he continued "they have to be filled with cash and then loaded on the trucks with the provisions slated for delivery to four different ships in port by tomorrow morning. There must be four bags per ship, delivered on time, and looking completely normal. Sal finally found out from his grandfather how the drug money was being sent out of the country on as regular a basis as the drugs were coming in. There are eight ships on various trans-pacific schedules on their way to Chile right now with millions of dollars on board stuffed into plain green duffel bags just like those. If we don't deliver these tomorrow without raising suspicions, we can kiss that entire amount of illegal money goodbye. Any hint of a problem and radio messages will go out from the sister ships in port to alert the Chilean shipping operation that the money transfer system has been compromised."

Sal's grandfather had, due to his age and health conditions, been released on a $2,000,000.00 cash bond pending his trial on the provision that he cooperate in the investigation. Bill had also been instrumental in having his former associate and errant family man, Chuck Rossi, released from his cell in Nanaimo on a similar basis. Chuck, in fact, was now providing valuable assistance in the warehouse to get the trucks loaded and ready for the Monday morning deliveries.

Sal had been gradually getting information from his grandfather on the workings of the special orders department, particularly when the old man finally became convinced that the legitimate part of the business would continue to operate under Sal's supervision. Strangely, he didn't seem to care much that his eldest grandson had been wounded and was in jail charged with murder. He had always thought that the boy had been crude and bad tempered.

As Sal had gleaned details of the QHRS operation in Chile and had learned the workings of the cash transfer and banking operations there, he soon realized that if the money chain were broken prematurely the managers in Chile would abandon the business and transfer the drug money to their own accounts in safe locations out of the country as fast as it arrived. He also had learned that Mr.Battista periodically sent senior people from Vancouver to audit the operation and make sure that no periodic management changes were necessary. Outgoing managers suspected of diverting cash from the business usually completely disappeared under very mysterious circumstances.

As Bill took up his new duties as a paper cutting professional, he was told that not only did they have to work as long as it took during the night to be sure that the trucks were loaded and

ready to roll first thing in the morning, but he also had to take
one of the delivery routes himself. He was also told to enjoy his
few hours off tomorrow evening after completing his deliveries,
because he was expected to be packed, dressed in his best suit,
and available at Vancouver International Airport at 7:00 a.m.
Tuesday morning.

Bill loudly expressed shock and dismay that he was flying
somewhere this close to his high school graduation day, until
he was firmly reminded that not only was his brain obviously
fatigued and not functioning well, but that his school activities
were his cover, not his career.

At this point, Bill quietly asked where it was they wanted
him to go. As the paper cutting and duffel bag stuffing exercises
continued at full speed, Inspector Hanley explained that he, Sal,
Bill, and Staff-Sergeant Rodriguez would be the QHRS Chilean
operations audit team this year. Sal would have a letter signed
by his grandfather appointing him as the senior management
auditor reporting directly to him for this purpose. Despite Sal's
youth, the management in Chile would respect the old man's
delegated authority since the consequences of past disobedience
were well known.

By 3:30 in the afternoon, the duffel bags were finally ready.
Three layers of $100 bills had been placed over the layers of blank
paper in each bag in case someone on one of the ships broke the
seal and slid the zipper down for a quick look. Inspector Hanley
had signed the money out of the evidence vault at "E" Division
Headquarters, thinking of the irony of putting the special orders
department profits right back to work in the business. With the
duffel bags ready, Bill and Sal began the real work of ensuring
that the route delivery trucks were properly loaded for the
morning. At one point during the frantically busy evening, Bill
took a break to call Allison and tell her that he would not be

able to see her until tomorrow after school. He asked her to have dinner with him so that he could tell her about his upcoming trip, the details of which he couldn't discuss over the phone.

The delivery trucks were completely loaded and ready to go by 11:00 p.m., so Sal and Bill were finally ready to leave, both well aware that they had to be back by 5:30 a.m. to begin the morning runs. Bill waved "goodnight," got in his aunt's car, and slowly drove home while he contemplated the hectic activities of his so-called Sunday off.

✸ Forty-five

John Cassidy dropped Bill off at the airport just before 6:00 a.m., wished him good luck and then continued back into Vancouver to go to work. Bill headed directly to the RCMP airport detachment office hoping to get a cup of coffee and a few minutes of quiet time before the rest of the team arrived. Corporal Kent greeted him with suspicion until he produced his ID and explained that he was part of Inspector Hanley's group. The corporal then brusquely told Bill that he was welcome to have some coffee if he made a fresh pot first.

As Bill busily found the filter and the coffee pack, filled the water jug and poured the contents into the coffee maker, he thought about his pleasant evening with Allison. As tired as he was when he finally got home from work yesterday, he perked up considerably when he found that his aunt had already done his packing for him. She had used his Uncle John's best suitcase so that he would look more like the businessman he was supposed to be. With that job done for him, he was able to quickly shower, change and rush out the door to walk the few blocks to meet Allison at the bus stop. He had convinced Allison to meet him away from the house so that he didn't have to reveal any details of his upcoming activities in the next two weeks to Sergeant Stuart.

After getting off the bus and settling into their booth at the White Spot Restaurant, Bill told Allison all about his impending trip to Chile the next morning which didn't engender a very positive response. Allison said that all of this police activity on Bill's part was new to her and very hard to get used to. Bill begged her to understand that this was part of the process of wrapping up this job, so that he could get on with the planning of their future life together. One of the delightful things about sharing a meal with Allison was the opportunity to sit directly opposite her at the table and look into her eyes as they talked. The trouble with doing that was the fact that he couldn't concentrate on what he was saying, so he had to keep on telling her how much he loved her instead. This led to a somewhat repetitive conversation, but Allison didn't seem to mind too much.

He was rudely awakened from his reminiscences when the detachment office door was suddenly pushed open and Sal, Gar Rodriguez and Inspector Hanley came in. This got Corporal Kent even more concerned about the invasion of his office by civilian intruders until the watch commander hurriedly appeared and warmly greeted the inspector.

After introductions all around, the sergeant produced a shoulder holster and a 9 mm Glock pistol for each one of the travelers. Sal declined his and said that he didn't have the slightest idea how to use it, and besides, weren't there three fine members of the force available to protect him? This seemed logical and Bill laughingly remarked that they would be in far more danger if Sal were armed than if he was not. This drew a nasty look from Corporal Kent, who still couldn't quite comprehend what this circus was all about and who these clowns really were.

The sergeant sent the group off to the ticket counter to check in for the flight and told them that he would meet them over by security. They were delighted to find that there was no line in front of the business class counter. They were even more delighted to find that their business class tickets to Santiago entitled them to be seated in first class on the initial flight to Los Angeles, where they would connect with the on-going flight for the rest of the trip to Chile. Having checked their bags and obtained their boarding passes, they went to the security inspection area entrance where the sergeant escorted them around the metal detectors. They were then led to the U.S. Customs and Immigration Service Inspection Area where the sergeant introduced them to the staff and indicated that they had been cleared for transit through LAX. After the Immigration Service Inspector made sure that they each had a valid passport, they were waved through to the gate waiting area.

Bill settled into his roomy seat and gazed around at his surroundings. This was a much bigger aircraft than anything that he had been on before and the seats were certainly more comfortable. Since he lucked out by having a window seat on the north side of the aircraft as it took off, he had a magnificent view of the North Shore Mountains as the plane sped down the runway and took off. After they had gained enough altitude to get above the clouds and reach level flight, he was able to take full advantage of the meal service. Then the fatigue factor from the last couple of days of frantic activity kicked in and he fell asleep.

Bill woke up with a start when the announcement to fasten their seat belts for arrival was supplemented by the flight attendant gently shaking his shoulder while asking him to prepare for the landing. He was astounded at the distance they had to taxi to the terminal building after landing at LAX and was amazed at the number of aircraft moving between the terminals and the taxiways. An FBI agent met them at the entrance to the jet way as they left the aircraft and escorted them through the terminal building to their departure gate for Santiago. Having boarded the aircraft and settled in, Bill once again enjoyed the take-off and the meal service, then resumed his interrupted sleep. He was vaguely aware of landing, sitting on the plane at some small airport somewhere and then taking off again around two in the morning. After trying to read for awhile, he gave up and continued his almost non-stop sleep to Chile.

⛭

Forty-six

As they climbed down the stairway that had been rolled up to the aircraft door, everybody could feel the heat and humidity as the sun rose in the eastern sky during their early morning arrival. They walked into the terminal building with the rest of the crowd and got into the lines for customs and immigration. Bill was acutely aware of the holster and weapon under his coat and hoped that he didn't end up in a Chilean jail cell because some alert agent noticed him. He soon realized that the arrival inspection was quite perfunctory, since the First and Business Class passengers were being processed first and the agents were not subjecting them to any delays. As they left the customs hall with their luggage, they quickly spotted a man in a chauffeur's uniform holding up a sign with **Senor Sal Battista** written in large black letters.

Sal was welcomed profusely, then they were led to a large, very spacious limousine complete with a bar refrigerator filled with juice and snacks. As the driver settled into his front seat, he was joined by a large individual in a similar uniform who was introduced as their bodyguard during their stay. Ernesto indicated that he was at their service, but they all felt that the service included keeping a very careful watch over them and everything that they did. They had been warned beforehand by the senior Mr. Battista not to say anything in the presence of the staff in Chile that they didn't want recorded and repeated. This included the limo, the guesthouse and particularly, the office and warehouse. Gar Rodriguez has also been warned not to reveal that he understood or spoke Spanish. He had already overheard the suspicious comment that Sal looked awfully young and inexperienced to be a senior member of the family that controlled the company.

The drive to Valparaiso from the Santiago Airport was uneventful and incredibly scenic once the city was left behind. If they had not been so tired after the long trip, they would have enjoyed it much more, but the comfort of the large limousine soon had everyone dozing again. In about an hour and a half they arrived at a mountain top compound with a ranch style mansion directly overlooking the city and the harbor far below. The compound was walled and contained a magnificent garden in the back of the house that offered floral scenery almost as spectacular as the harbor view in front. As the limousine entered the gate and rolled up to the wide porch at the front door, a butler and a housekeeper emerged to greet them.

As introductions were made by Ernesto, it was obvious that the housekeeper had assumed that Inspector Hanley was the esteemed Senor Battista and it took a flurried conversation in español before she realized that young Sal was indeed the senior family member who was the company manager. When this was settled, they were escorted to their rooms, with Sal being led to the large corner suite with the harbor view. It was suggested that they all rest until lunch at 1:00 p.m., at which time they could meet the managing director for Chilean operations who would be most interested to learn of their proposed agenda for the visit.

Jorge Estaban was seated in the small reception area just outside the dining room when Sal arrived from his room. After slowly getting to his feet with a slight hint of impatience, he introduced himself and assured Sal that everything was in readiness for the audit. Just then, Mike Hanley, Bill, and Gar straggled in and the introductions began all over again. The housekeeper then ushered them into the dining room where a white-jacketed waiter was filling the wine glasses with a fine Chilean white wine. The dining room was elegantly furnished with a burnished mahogany table with seating for at least twenty, a huge matching sideboard, a china cabinet with indirect interior lighting and a magnificent compliment of English china.

After they were seated, Senor Estaban offered a welcoming toast, which Mike responded to on behalf of all of the senior management and staff of the corporate office. Mike emphasized how honored they were that the new CEO, Executive Vice President Battista, had taken the time from his busy schedule to accompany the management audit team to Chile and secretly chuckled at the confusion on Estaban's face as he learned of Sal's new title and responsibilities for the first time. Mike went on to explain that the venerable Guido Battista had decided to skip an entire generation of family management and place the operation of the company directly into Sal's capable hands. The management team, of course, was entirely committed to support this wise decision.

While Jorge Estaban urbanely listened to Mike's explanation, his eyes had turned cold and decidedly unfriendly as the discussion continued. While outwardly affable and friendly, to the trained observer it was apparent that he was very annoyed that his intelligence connections in the head office had not informed him of this sweeping change in control. Of course, he had no particular way of knowing that all of his trusted contacts in Vancouver were being held in a cellblock with no access to communications of any sort.

As lunch was being served, Senor Estaban outlined his plans for their visit, beginning with an afternoon tour of the Valparaiso Region and its magnificent harbor; a cocktail reception at 7:00 p.m. to meet the local QHRS management team; followed by dinner and dancing to a string quartet that featured local contemporary music. A number of very accommodating senoritas had also been invited to enhance their evening recreation. A plant indoctrination tour would begin at 10:00 a.m. tomorrow, after lunch followed by the usual presentations by the various company department heads.

Sal expressed his thanks for the hospitality and then detailed what the real agenda was going to be. The afternoon tour was acceptable but there would be a quiet early dinner for the audit team only, since a complete top-to-bottom inspection of the entire QHRS facility would begin at 6:00 a.m. tomorrow. This initial inspection by the entire team would be followed by individual team members conducting in-depth audits of the various operating departments. Mr. Hanley would review the financial operations and inspect the books and banking records. Mr. Patterson would review the warehouse, shipping, receiving and waterborne transportation operations, while he, Mr. Battista, accompanied by Mr. Rodriguez would audit the special orders department.

Estaban could barely conceal his fury as he protested Sal's plan, indicating that there would be nothing to see at 6:00 a.m., and that the department managers couldn't be expected to have their presentations ready on such short notice. Mike responded that the warehouse should be in full operation by that time of morning if company guidelines were being followed, and further more, no presentations by department heads were required, only immediate response to questions asked and prompt presentation of any requested documents. This was not some sort of management presentation exercise followed by a question and answer period, but an in-depth audit with documented evidence of an efficient operation and valid reasons why business should continue to be conducted in the present way. The team had to be prepared to recommend to the corporate board of directors that things continue as found, or present an alternate plan to improve operations should that be warranted. Senor Estaban was stunned and loudly indicated that he couldn't tolerate such an approach and the insults that were implied. Sal cheerfully indicated that he would be happy to accept a resignation if that was what the senor wanted, otherwise the audit would proceed exactly as outlined by Mr. Hanley.

Forty-seven

At exactly 5:45 a.m. Ernesto opened the rear door of the limousine for Sal, while the others climbed into the remaining back seats. The drive down the hillside into the city was beautiful at first light with the rising sun behind them already illuminating the harbor and the ships slowly swinging around on their anchor chains as the tide changed. The group said very little during the drive, each wondering quietly how the day would go and what would be found.

Last evening after dinner the four of them, drinks in hand, had strolled through the rear garden admiring the flowering trees and brilliant well-tended planters on the spacious grounds. It was their only opportunity to talk openly without concerns about being recorded, and even at that, they talked quietly and directly to each other for fear of directional boom microphones on the roof of the hacienda. They went over their plans for the next day and pondered their approach to taking control of the facility later in the week. As they entered the spacious lobby of QHRS–Valparaiso, wearing their finest suits to create the impression that they really were successful business men, they were met by a glowering Senor Estaban and three other individuals who looked like hired thugs obviously not impressed with their gringo visitors.

"Good morning, Jorge," Sal said cheerfully, "this is our plan for the morning. Bill and Gar will begin in the warehouse right now, Mike needs to be taken to accounting and finance, and I would like to go to the executive offices, meet the rest of your staff and then proceed to special orders." Estaban curtly gave orders in Spanish and one of the associates motioned Bill and Gar to follow him through the large double doors leading to the warehouse offices. Bill glanced back and saw Sal and Mike being led to the elevator on the other side of the lobby. He instinctively patted himself to ensure that his weapon was in place under his jacket, then immediately regretted his action which was totally counter to his training that emphasized not revealing what you might be carrying.

As it turned out, Bill had a very enjoyable morning since the warehouse operation was exceptionally well run and extremely efficient. Trucks were arriving constantly from the outlying regions of the country to the receiving docks, where crews unloaded them promptly taking the flats of succulent fresh fruit and vegetables to the conveyors where washing and grading took place. Inspectors carefully reviewed the process lines where flash cooling and loading into the refrigerated containers took place. As each container was filled the door was closed and locked and the temperature and humidity recorded. Then the containers were moved swiftly to the loading docks and onto the flatbed trucks that would proceed to the piers and then directly down to the ship's side for loading.

Bill estimated that, since the trucks had driven all night having been loaded on the farm the previous evening, less than twelve hours was required for the produce to move from being freshly picked to being loaded onto the ship in containers set at just the right temperature to maintain the cargo in farm fresh condition upon arrival in Vancouver. He was very impressed and made sure that the warehouse superintendent knew that he would receive very high marks in the inspection report to Mr. Battista.

Bill also noted that there was a mini-version of the Vancouver operation, whereby trucks were loaded with a variety of foods for delivery to local hotels and restaurants, but it was obvious that processing fresh cargo for delivery to Vancouver by ship was the key function of this facility. While Bill had been working exclusively with Jose Ortega, the warehouse superintendent, Gar had the opportunity to stroll around the warehouse perimeters and talk to the drivers, helpers and warehouse workers about their jobs and relationships with top management. While everyone spoke highly of Senor Ortega, they would not discuss their feelings about the higher management levels at all. Gar sensed a real uneasiness about any discussions regarding that group.

Mike Hanley also had a positive morning in as much as the Director of Finance, Senor Manuel Sotos, was a young, very earnest manager with an in-depth knowledge of proper accounting practices and a real eye for bottom line results. Mike's questions were answered promptly and without hesitation. Financial information and documentation was produced just as soon as it was requested and it became obvious to Mike that not only was the business being run in a profitable, professional, manner but that the finances associated with the special orders department were not being handled by this organization. He was secretly quite pleased that, once again, the legitimate part of the business was capable of continuing profitable operation without the enormous illegal revenue from special orders. The real trick lay in coming up with a scheme to separate them, since they had no criminal justice system back up in Chile. In fact, there was a very good chance that both federal and local police support would be for the perpetrators, not the legitimate owners of the company.

Sal was not having a good morning. He had been grudgingly

ushered into the extravagantly decorated and furnished executive offices on the top floor. The conference room was huge with all kinds of electronic projection equipment, laptops at every other chair and extensive telephone conference calling capability. Sal was convinced that it also had significant listening and recording capabilities. He had been waved towards a chair in the middle, but he immediately went to the head of the table and sat down. After waiting in silence for a minute or two with no offer of coffee or juice forthcoming, he demanded that a tray of coffee and biscuits be brought in. One of Jorge's henchmen opened a door to the adjoining pantry and barked out an order. Shortly thereafter a middle-aged woman appeared and set out cups, saucers and small plates in front of the participants. She then commenced filling coffee cups, starting with Estaban and his managers, and finishing up with Sal. She didn't look as though she enjoyed her job at all, but that may have been partly due to the early morning hour.

"Gentlemen," Sal began. "I am the principal owner and Chief Executive Officer of the Quality Hotel and Restaurant Supply Company and it's worldwide operations, the designated successor of my esteemed grandfather, Guido Battista. I intend to continue the successful and profitable operation of this company without major changes, but I demand unconditional loyalty from all employees and in particular the senior managers who have been highly rewarded in the past for all of their efforts. Any lesser level of respect and commitment from that which has always been offered to my grandfather will result in immediate replacement. If that is clear I would like you, going around the table in turn, to introduce yourselves and explain exactly what your duties are in the QHRS-Chile operation."

While this statement was being considered in stunned silence, the pantry door opened and Gar Rodriguez strolled in, casually helped himself to a cup of coffee and a couple of cookies, then sat down near Sal. Just as casually, he took his weapon out of the shoulder holster beneath his jacket and laid it on the table in front of him. Then he grinned and invited them to continue the session just as Mr. Battista had requested.

During the working lunch in the conference room, which Sal had insisted on despite Estaban's protests that it was barbaric to try to eat while working, both Bill and Mike joined the group for lunch and gave glowing reports about the segments of the business records that they had reviewed. Sal then indicated that the special orders department financial status seemed to be outstanding as reported, but he now considered it imperative that they collectively observe the workings of the operation.

Having been led from the lobby through two sets of doors with cipher locks, the team entered the first large processing area of the department. Adjacent to a separate set of receiving and shipping docks, dozens of packages were brought in from certain trucks that had been moved here after being initially unloaded at the other end of the warehouse. The packages were sorted into the cocaine and heroin processing lines, weighed, emptied, inspected, and repackaged into one kilo bags. Further along the line, the bags were packed into small duffel bags, completely filling them. These were then sealed and wrapped in plastic. Two small duffel bags were then packed into a large duffel bag, which contained an outer layer of foam flotation material. These were also sealed and plastic wrapped with a tiny radio beacon transmitter attached. The prepared duffel bags were given serial number tags, weighed, recorded and moved out to QHRS delivery trucks that had already been loaded with provisions for delivery to cargo ships in the harbor. Guards armed with machine pistols were located at every entrance to the processing room and others coldly observed the work in progress at each station. Any attempt to pilfer the product would result in instant death.

Bill estimated that whole process was just as efficient as the work done at the other end of the warehouse complex and told Jorge that he had very efficient operating teams. Jorge seemed to be warming up to the entire inspection process, but his subordinate managers didn't relax or indicate that they were happy in any way at all. They continued to subject the visitors to intense inspection, glowering when anything that was said didn't please them. They continued to exchange muttered comments to each other in Spanish, which Sal profoundly hoped that Gar overheard.

The inspection team was then escorted through two more sets of cipher lock doors into the next processing area. Here, packed duffel bags were brought in from ships in the harbor by trucks arriving at another adjacent loading dock. Several parallel conveyor lines were in operation where the bag contents were dumped onto the slowly moving belts, the piles of currency spread out, and workers quickly moved the bills onto other belts based on denomination. These belts unloaded separate streams of 100, fifty, twenty and ten dollar bills into canvas bank deposit bags. Each filled bag was then moved to the counting tables where two workers at each table counted and recorded the amounts, then sealed the bags. The bank deposit bags were then loaded into produce boxes with attractive labels marked fresh carrots, lettuce, etc., and taken to the loading dock where, it was explained, regular QHRS delivery trucks stopped off at various banks on their regular routes to make deposits. Each bank had been led to believe that they were the sole depository for the company in Valpairaiso. The large duffel bags, which had been emptied, were finally taken next door to the drug-processing workroom to begin the cycle again. Once again, Bill remarked to Jorge on the efficiency of the operation and once again the other managers glowered at him. The well-armed guards didn't take their eyes off of him for a second. Sal had the distinct impression that CEO or not, one move to inspect even a twenty-dollar bill would have resulted in a hail of bullets being fired at him.

At this point, Sal announced that he didn't wish to have his audit team disrupt the normal routine any longer today and suggested that they return to the lobby. Once back in the lobby, he requested that the limousine be brought to the door and told Jorge and the others that the team would return promptly at 10:00 a.m. the next morning to wrap up the audit for the year. The concession given to start the next management day at a more civilized hour resulted in a few wan smiles, but no friendly handshakes were offered to end the visit.

Forty-eight

Mike had requested that Ernesto take them on a tour around the waterfront after leaving the QHRS complex, expressing a desire to see the docks where the refrigerated containers were loaded onto the ships. They spent over an hour covering various areas of the harbor that turned out to be very informative and interesting. They were not able to go near the naval piers, which were closed to the public in preparation for some foreign ship visits scheduled for the next day.

After an early dinner at the hacienda, they took after-dinner drinks into the garden and strolled around enjoying the last glimpse of the setting sun over the harbor far below. Their quiet conversations revealed that everyone was impressed with the QHRS-Chile operation, particularly the criminal side of things, and were terrified that they had no apparent means of stopping the activities before the large shipments of dollar-sized blank paper were delivered from the ships that were just days away from arrival. It was obvious that at the first hint of trouble the operation would suddenly close down with millions of dollars in cash and drugs disappearing forever. A sudden closing would also destroy the legitimate side of the business, cutting off a major supply line to the Vancouver warehouse and the distribution system.

226

Mike had no access to police help, the RCMP presence in the Canadian Embassy in Santiago was far too small to do any good and they had absolutely no legal basis to conduct a police raid in Chile anyway. Mike was sure that the local authorities were part of the business, since no operation of this size could operate undetected even with generous bribes. It was much more likely that ten to fifteen percent of the profits went directly to the police commissioner each day for distribution to the lesser police officials.

So they strolled and worried, and worried and strolled, until they were very tired and decided to call it a night. Just as they had returned their glasses to the kitchen and headed down the hall to the bedrooms, Mike stopped in his tracks. He excitedly motioned them to follow him, then headed back out to the garden and moved quickly to the far end. Of course the video monitors picked them up, but the microphones could not detect the lively conversations that ensued. Mike had suddenly realized what he had seen as they got out of the limousine after returning from their harbor tour. Coming into the harbor entrance in the glow of the late afternoon sun was the arriving line of visiting warships which were the subject of the preparation at the naval piers. And Mike was convinced that the last ship in the line he had seen was a Canadian frigate.

In the morning, Mike was out the front door and into the taxi that he had called from his bedroom telephone before Ernesto realized that anyone was even up. Since the taxi pulled away immediately, he had no time to arrange for anyone to follow, so all he could do was call Jorge and report what had happened. He did try to question Sal in an off-hand way about the whereabouts of Senor Hanley, but Sal was not about to explain their activities to anyone.

Mike paid the taxi driver including a generous tip which he

hoped would also buy his silence for a little while, then walked down the pier to the last ship in line. The Chilean Navy sentry obviously though that Mike was just returning to his ship after a night on the town and had passed him through the gate after an ID card had been waved in his general direction. He marched up the brow to the quarterdeck of *HMCS Vancouver*, came to attention facing the colors, then turned and told the Boatswain of the Watch that he wished to see the commanding officer. He was brusquely advised that visiting hours were not until 10:00 a.m. and that he would have to come back then. Mike then asked to speak to the officer of the day. Lieutenant Kim Parker had completed her morning rounds after assuming the duty and had just finished pouring a cup of coffee when the wardroom phone ran. The BM advised her that a visitor was at the brow and was insisting on seeing the CO. Kim sighed, put down her cup and headed for the quarterdeck thinking along the way that this was just the beginning of a very long, busy day.

When Lieutenant Parker approached, Mike took her out of the hearing of the boatswain and introduced himself as Inspector Hanley of the RCMP, showing her his ID card as he did so. She asked him to wait while she telephoned the CO, then after a brief conversation, directed him to follow her into the interior of the ship and up the ladder to the CO's cabin. Cdr. David Miles had hastily put on his uniform jacket, asked the steward to make a fresh pot of coffee and then met Mike at his cabin door. Mike introduced himself, showed his ID card once again and asked if they could talk for a few minutes about an urgent on-going investigation. Thirty minutes later, the executive officer was called to the cabin, followed by the weapons officer and finally, by the supply officer. Another thirty minutes of conversation took place, then Mike left the ship, walked up the pier and found another taxi to take him to QHRS.

Mike entered the QHRS boardroom thirty minutes late, apologizing to Sal for his tardiness, but indicated that he had good news for all of them. Sal indicated that he had arrived just in time to give his impressions of the local accounting and finance operations, since Bill had just concluded the discussions on warehousing and delivery. Mike summarized his review, made suggestions for improved internal audits that were well received, and then announced that he had visited *HMCS Vancouver* early this morning. He also revealed that he had discovered an old acquaintance of his commanded the ship and that all QHRS management personnel were invited to the reception and cocktail party to be held on board from 8:00 to 10:00 p.m. that evening. Sal expressed delight that the invitation included the senior Chilean management of a well respected Canadian owned company and insisted that Jorge and his associates clear their calendars to ensure that everyone would be there to meet and mingle with the other dignitaries and business owners from the surrounding community.

Forty-nine

I t was a beautiful evening, warm with a gentle breeze blowing across the harbor. The four naval ships at the pier were all cheerfully illuminated by the decorative lighting fixtures strung from the bow up to the masthead and down again to the stern. A large, canvas awning had been installed above the entire helicopter deck of *HMCS Vancouver*, transforming the area into a very large reception hall with a buffet dinner line laid out fore and aft on one side of the deck and a very long bar on the other. Low-level decorative lighting had also been installed under the awning, giving the whole area a festive touch. A string quartet, composed of volunteer crew members with musical talent, was playing in the background. The musicians were already looking forward to their break when they could sample the food and have a glass of wine or two as a small reward for their service.

Cdr. Miles and his senior officers in their evening dress uniforms were moving amongst the prominent local guests, chatting and making sure that they were looked after by the stewards circulating with trays of hors-d' ouvres and glasses of wine. Other officers were entertaining the visitors from the other ships at the pier, ensuring that they knew that both the bar and the serving line were open and available, while exchanging the latest jokes and sea stories. Lieutenant Parker with the boatswain of the watch, were on the quarterdeck forward greeting visitors as they stepped aboard and inviting people to sign the ship's guest book before going aft to the party.

Sal, Mike, Gar and Bill were on the pier greeting Jorge and his six senior managers as they stepped out of the limousine, Ernesto having been instructed to pick them up at their homes and bring them to the ship. Sal, in particular, was enthusiastic in his greetings being particularly pleased, as he told them, that QHRS would be so well represented at this influential gathering. After signing the guest book at Kim Parker's urging, having coyly mentioned that she was always interested in getting the phone numbers of such special visitors, they proceeded to the flight deck to join the festivities. Sal led them into the midst of the crowd, introducing them to Cdr. Miles who welcomed them enthusiastically and pointed out the locations of the bar and the buffet serving line, inviting them to help themselves.

Jorge and his managers lost no time in mingling with the other guests from the Valparaiso business community, many of whom they knew. As the evening progressed, they also tried to spend quality time mingling with the newly commissioned female acting sub-lieutenants who were graciously serving drinks to the more senior guests. Having been very well trained, these junior officers lost no time in letting these "honored guests" know that they were not at all impressed with their approach or their manners. Mike, in the meantime, had cornered the ambassador and the naval attaché and was quietly outlining the real plans for the rest of the evening and the next day. The ambassador was really concerned about the reaction from the Chilean Government officials when they found out about what was going to happen and urged Mike to be extremely cautious. He also strongly suggested that the attaché call Ottawa and ensure that appropriate orders were issued to the ship to sail earlier than originally planned. In fact, in his opinion, the ship should leave Chile just as soon as Mike had completed his work

Shortly after 9:30 p.m., Manuel Soto and Jose Ortega approached Sal and Mike to ask if they could be excused early since tomorrow was a regular working day and they both had to be at the warehouse first thing in the morning to get things off to a good start. Sal agreed, of course, and asked them both to meet him in the executive conference room at 9:30 a.m. tomorrow morning. Manuel cast an anxious glance in the direction of Jorge and then asked if Sal was sure that it was he that he wanted to see. Sal said yes, Manuel and Jose were exactly the people he wanted to talk to, not the others. At this point, Mike had Ernesto called to the quarterdeck from the petty officers' mess where he had been enjoying some light refreshments and asked him to drive Manuel and Jose home, indicating that the rest of them would find there own way home by taxi later on. Sal then asked Ernesto to pick them up at the hacienda at 9:00 a.m. for the usual trip to the office.

Shortly after 10:00 p.m., as the majority of the guests were thanking Cdr. Miles and offering their farewells, Sal approached Jorge and his group who were still trying to impress the young female officers with their accomplishments in the business world and who were feeling quite pleased with themselves by this time. Sal indicated that they had been further honored by an invitation to attend a smaller, private, reception in the wardroom and asked everyone to accompany Mike down below. As they cheerfully tramped down the ladders and along the passageway into the wardroom lounge, they were directed by Gar to have a seat while the steward filled their coffee cups. They weren't too thrilled by the offer of coffee, but obediently sat down anyway.

After the coffee had been poured, the steward and everyone else but Mike and Gar left the room. As Jorge and the others looked puzzled, two armed petty officers took up station just inside the door and Mike announced that he was Inspector Michael Hanley, Royal Canadian Mounted Police and they were under arrest. He explained their rights and emphasized that since they were presently onboard a Canadian naval ship, they were under Canadian jurisdiction. Mike and Gar then proceeded to check them for weapons and produced quite a selection of concealed pistols and knives which were handed over for tagging and storage by the chief petty officer who had appeared just for that purpose.

Mike then announced that Staff Sergeant Gar Rodriguez would read the list of formal charges to each of the five men in turn and indicated that the proceeding was being tape recorded for the record and that copies of the tapes would be given to their attorneys of choice in Vancouver as well as to the Crown Attorney. Jorge vehemently objected to the whole idea and stood up to leave the wardroom, cursing wildly and pushing past Gar as he headed for the door. One of the petty officers none to gently propelled him back into his seat as the other petty officer with weapon drawn, warned the other four to stay where they were. Gar, using the full names and local addresses recorded by each of them in the quarterdeck guest book, solemnly read an extensive list of charges to each person in turn, reminding them that no response was necessary at the present time.

After the charges had been formally read, the five men were told to strip to their underwear and were given sets of blue coveralls to put on while their clothing and personal possessions were being collected under the watchful eye of the guards. Mike explained that they would be confined in a six person berthing compartment for the trip to Vancouver under armed guard at all times. They would not be permitted to communicate with anyone until their arrival in Vancouver. Sal would arrange for attorneys to represent them on arrival if they did not have anyone of their own in mind. Their families would be advised sometime tomorrow morning that they had been called away on business. Amidst much cursing, swearing and threats of extreme violence both in English and in Spanish, they were hustled away to their accommodations for the duration of their unintentional West Coast cruise.

Fifty

Promptly at 8:00 a.m., five QHRS refrigerated trucks arrived at the naval pier to deliver fresh provisions to the visiting ships. While one truck went to each of the three USN ships, two of them stopped at the brow of *HMCS Vancouver*, prompting the supply officers on the other ships to question aloud why *Vancouver* needed so much more than the rest of the squadron. Some joker in the crowd offered that since Canadian ships were still civilized enough to have a wardroom bar, the second truck obviously was there to replenish the liquor.

Vancouver's boatswain piped the duty watch to the brow to assemble a work party to unload the trucks. As the lines formed passing the cartons and crates from the truck doors, up the gangway and forward to the storerooms, the drivers were invited to the mess deck for morning coffee. Once the drivers were down below and out of sight, two highly trained and well-armed ships' boarding teams wearing black coveralls and knit watch caps scurried to the trucks and quickly climbed into the cargo compartments that had just been emptied. As a courtesy, Bill turned off the reefer compressors before closing the doors. With Bill and Gar driving, the two trucks left the navy pier and headed back to the warehouse, intentionally leaving the regular drivers behind. After a slow and convoluted trip to the warehouse, primarily caused by Gar getting lost several times trying to navigate through the roadways servicing the waterfront dock complex, they arrived at the QHRS special orders loading bay area.

After backing the trucks into empty bays, Bill at the currency handling section and Gar at the drug processing operation, opened the truck cargo doors. The fourteen person ship boarding teams, led by their Officer-In-Charge, quickly moved to either side of a warehouse loading door at each location. Gar loudly banged on the door at the drug processing location and called out something in Spanish.

As the small personnel entrance door in the large loading bay door opened and a suspicious guard peered out, weapon in hand, he was suddenly grabbed, pulled through the door, disarmed, and thrown to the ground to be quickly bound, gagged and put into the back of the truck. After a few seconds another guard appeared, looking for the previous one and soon was in the truck with his associate. One by one a guard would look out and then be hustled away while the work continued inside the processing room. With no senior managers present, there was a relaxed atmosphere and nobody was paying much attention to what was going on at the side doors. There was no rush to finish the day's work of packing all the duffel bags ready for loading into the trucks and the workers anticipated payday and a day off. No one even speculated as to why there were no managers present, it was so pleasant to work without the insults, harassment, and the shouted obscenities that normally filled their working days.

When the similar activities at the other loading dock had been completed, the well-armed boarding teams quietly resumed their places inside the warehouse, glowering at everybody as usual. Gar was profoundly hoping that no one spoke to them, since these newly recruited security professionals in borrowed ill fitting uniforms spoke little or no Spanish.

Sal and Mike entered the building lobby just after 9:20 a.m. and took the elevator directly to the fourth floor executive offices. As they moved down the hall to the conference room, they were confronted by an angry Senora Mendez, who informed them that they could not use the room without the permission of Senor Estaban. Sal then quietly but firmly reminded Senora Mendez that he was the CEO of QHRS, not Senor Estaban. He also requested that a pot of fresh coffee and a tray of suitable biscuits be brought to the conference room for his morning management meeting.

Manuel Soto and Jose Ortega entered the conference room where they were warmly greeted by Mike Hanley. Sal had to go back out to the executive floor lobby to get them past Senora Mendez, who seemingly had forgotten the previous message and was loudly proclaiming that they were not permitted on this floor unless specifically invited by Senor Estaban. Sal came in after them, closed the door, and invited them to sit down and have some coffee. Mike then slipped out through the pantry, went quietly down the hall and caught the Senora putting a fresh tape into a recording machine on her desk. Mike pulled out the wires and threw the machine into a nearby wastebasket which resulted in a resounding crash and a gasp of horror from Senora Mendez.

Mike then returned to the room, poured himself a cup of coffee and listened as Sal began to explain to Manuel and Jose what had recently happened to the company operation in Vancouver. He summarized the demise of the criminal side of the business and was happy to announce that the legitimate, traditional operations were being permitted to continue by the RCMP with the concurrence of the BC Provincial Prosecutor's Office and the courts. He then went on to introduce Inspector Hanley, RCMP, to the astounded pair of local managers.

Sal and Mike had spent well over an hour providing the

background on the recent company activities before coming to the real question, "Would Manuel Soto be willing to assume the post of QHRS-Chile General Manager with Jose Ortega as the Assistant General manager and Superintendent of Operations?"

Mike outlined the dangers associated with the job, particularly in withstanding the pressure from local officials and the local law enforcement officers. There was also the job of admitting to the families of Jorge Estaban and his associates that they had all been arrested and taken to Canada for trial. All of this after Sal and his team had left the country.

Both men seemed sincere in their desire to assume the responsibility, provided that the illegal part of the operation was permanently shut down, so Sal outlined the organizational and reporting relationships and advised them of the salaries that he was prepared to pay.

After recovering from their very pleasant surprise and agreeing that there were good, competent, people in the local organization that could be promoted into their present jobs, both men signed two-year employment contracts and agreed to keep the new arrangements confidential until Sal and the group were safely on their way home. Mike then indicated that checks for three months severance pay should be prepared immediately for the employees in the special orders department and Manuel telephoned the necessary instructions to the payroll department. Sal requested that Jose Ortega have four empty trucks moved to the special operations loading bays, then send the drivers back to their regular jobs. At this point, Mike suggested that he and Sal had best go downstairs to see how Bill and Gar were doing.

Sal first went down the hall and invited Senora Mendez into the room. He told her that while Senor Estaban and his senior management associates were away having a well-deserved rest, which, incidentally, included a company paid cruise. Senor Soto would be acting on his behalf as general manager. The Senora was told to provide whatever assistance Senor Soto requested in the day-to-day management of the organization.

Fiifty-one

Sal and Mike stopped in frustration after realizing that they had no idea what the codes were for opening the access doors from the lobby to the special orders department. That meant that they had to go outside to the loading bays, walk down to the appropriate door and enter the facility that way after finally convincing the sailors from the *Vancouver* that they had legitimate business inside. Bill had to be quietly summoned to vouch for them and he indicated to the troops that despite their suspicious looks and shifty ways they really were pretty good guys. This earned Bill an exasperated look from his commanding officer who was in no position just then to say anything in return.

The frantic daily routine in the drug packaging operations was winding down since all of the duffel bags were packed and ready for transport to the loading docks. The foreman had been waiting for the management order to begin loading, but with no manager there, he had not been sure what to do. Using Gar to translate, Sal issued the order to have the bags loaded onto the empty trucks that were waiting directly outside instead of the usual delivery trucks at the food warehouse end of the building. Sal and Gar then moved to the currency handling area and found that all of the money bags processed today had been neatly packed into the produce boxes and were ready for loading. The foreman there had also been waiting for his orders to begin loading the trucks and Sal relayed the same instructions as before.

Once the loading had been completed under the extremely vigilant scrutiny of the guards, weapons pointed and ready for anything, the trucks left for the piers with the *HMCS Vancouver* personnel driving. Mike and Bill rode along in the lead trucks of each section. Sal then had Gar assemble all special operations personnel in one large area and asked Manuel Soto to announce that starting immediately all employees of the two warehouse sections were being given three months off with pay. While the surprised workers loudly questioned each other about the meaning of all of this, payroll department employees started distributing the salary checks to the crowd. At this point Gar announced that everyone could leave as soon as they had received their checks and had picked up their belongings. The guards, weapons at the ready as usual, came in to watch and make sure that everyone left the building without a disturbance.

Later, after the payroll department employees had returned to work and a thorough search of the entire special operations complex had been completed to ensure that no one else was left inside, the officers-in-charge of the boarding party teams had their personnel free the regular guards and bring them into the warehouse. Manuel made the same announcement to them, and personally gave each man his check along with a cash bonus. Gar offered an apology for the way that the company security audit team had treated them, while at the same time berating them for being so unprepared that the audit team had easily gotten the better of them. He wished them well during their time off and indicated that all weapons would be securely locked away until the company operations began again. Gar then asked the boarding teams to do another search of the complex, turn off all the lights in that part of the warehouse at the circuit breaker panels and then lock every door leading to and from the area.

As the ship teams boarded the trucks to return to the *Vancouver*, Sal and Gar walked with Manuel back to his office and asked him if he was still ready to take over the management of the operation. After receiving assurances that he was, Sal said that he and Gar would be leaving for the rest of the day but would be back in the morning to answer any final questions that might come up before leaving for the airport.

By the time that Ernesto had brought the limousine around to the front entrance to pick up Sal and Gar, all six trucks had arrived at the ship. And by the time that Sal and Gar arrived there, the entire ship's company under the watchful supervision of Commander Miles and the XO were passing very heavy duffel bags from the trucks, up the brow, through the ship and down into the magazines where it had been decided to store them. In addition, the disguised boxes containing the cash were loaded aboard. Upon completion of this activity, Bill and Mike came off the ship, the brow was lifted to the pier and sentries were posted on the upper decks. At David Miles' request, the USN ships had posted a Marine security detail at the head of the pier which was refusing entry to any one other than personnel returning from liberty. The Chilean Naval sentry at the pier was puzzled by this new activity, but wisely declined to question the determined looking guard detail just inside the gate. Shortly after this, a convoy of empty QHRS trucks led by Ernesto in the limousine traveled back to the warehouse where they were met by Jose Ortega who directed them into the normal overnight parking spots. The two regular drivers who had spent most of the day on the ship rushed up to Jose trying to explain their absence from work due to the almost unending hospitality of the ship's force. Jose told them that they had done very well by socializing with the good customers and assured them that they were not in any kind of trouble.

Fifty-two

Around 7:30 a.m. the next morning a taxi from the Santiago Airport arrived at the ship with three weary looking people in Canadian naval uniforms. Having gotten off the long direct flight from Los Angeles, the three petty officers explained to the bored Chilean Immigration Officer that they were naval reserve personnel assigned to *HMCS Vancouver* for training. After being waved through customs and going outside, they finally found a taxi driver who understood enough English to realize that they wanted to be taken to Valpariaso.

After reporting on board and having some wake-up coffee in the mess, they went to their assigned berthing space and changed into their working uniforms. This immediately identified them as the RCMP corporal and two constables who were charged with the safe custody of many millions of dollars worth of drugs and millions of dollars in cash that was piled up in the evidence locker. This was the locker that used to have a single purpose as the main gun ammunition magazine. They also assumed the responsibility for the cruise passengers who comprised the former top management of QHRS-Chile. Chief Superintendent Singh had felt that it was unfair to Commander Miles and his crew to have this additional responsibility when they also had a ship to run. The XO willingly issued them side arms from the small arms

244

locker, since they had not wanted to risk carrying weapons into the country when traveling as naval personnel in uniform.

Mike, Bill and Gar arrived on board for a hurried last minute conference while the ship was preparing to get underway. The rest of the squadron was also cutting their port visit short in support of the Canadian Ambassador's request to get the hell out of port before the local officials discovered what was really going on. The United States Ambassador to Chile not only supported the move, but also sent a squad of Marines from the Embassy to take over pier sentry duty while the ships got underway.

Shortly after Mike and the others had settled into the limousine for the return trip to the office to meet Sal, an ornate official vehicle with blaring siren closely followed by a truck filled with well-armed policemen arrived at the pier gate. Mike told Ernesto to get a move on just as the police commissioner ordered the Marines at the gate to step aside. While the commissioner ranted and raved in front of the stoic Marine staff sergeant heading the guard detail that blocked the access to the pier, the cruiser flying the pennant of the squadron commander started moving away from the pier and headed towards the harbor entrance. Close behind were an Aegis destroyer, a Perry Class frigate and *HMCS Vancouver.*

The commissioner screamed at the ships to stop and ordered his people to open fire, which they did with little effect other than to see the four ships accelerate even more rapidly while leaving the harbor behind. The commissioner bellowed orders on his radio and a police patrol boat began to speed out towards the departing ships in a futile effort to stop them. Shortly after that, a pair of fighter jets appeared to dive towards the squadron and then hastily pulled up as the targeting radar for air defense missiles on four different ships locked onto them. As the aircraft disappeared, the squadron reached the outer harbor limits and began to turn north towards home.

As Mike, Bill, and Gar were getting out of the limousine at the office, having once again dressed for the occasion in their best suits, Mike asked Ernesto to return for them at 4:00 p.m. He also asked Ernesto to tell the housekeeper that they would all be returning to Vancouver tomorrow morning, and requested that the limousine be available for a trip to the airport around 10:00 a.m. At their wrap-up meeting with Manuel and Jose in the conference room, Mike advised them to have all of the drivers who did the overnight runs bringing in the produce from the countryside to refuse to accept any more drug shipments. They should also return anything that they had brought in recently to its source on their next trip out. The explanation should be that a big raid had occurred yesterday with the seizure of all of the drugs and money in the warehouse. They should also be told that no more money would be coming from them as the raiders had taken it all. There was no need to tell the company drivers about who had conducted the raid, let everyone speculate about that.

Manuel was also asked to quietly find the many QHRS bank accounts in which the drug money had been deposited and discretely close them. The money from any illegitimate company accounts should be taken to the security officer at the Canadian Embassy. Mike also warned Manuel that he could expect a raid by the local police at any time, but the crew from the *Vancouver* under Gar's direction had already thoroughly searched the special orders areas and thrown anything suspicious in dumpsters down the alley from the plant.

Sal then announced that it was time to say "goodbye" and profusely thanked Manuel and Jose once again for agreeing to take on the local management responsibilities. He promised to return in six months to see how things were going and begged them to phone him regularly to keep him up to date on the operation. Mike then asked if they could have a truck take everyone to the airport in Santiago now, before a serious search for them could begin. Jose immediately offered to drive them himself since he had the necessary identification to get the truck into the airport loading areas on the pretext of making a delivery to the flight kitchens.

Bill produced an empty grapefruit box that he had picked up in the warehouse and the three RCMP personnel produced all of their concealed weapons and placed them in the box. When the box had been taped up and Jose had signed a receipt for it to keep the administrators happy, Mike requested that the box also be delivered to the embassy security officer for shipment to Vancouver by diplomatic pouch. They all felt suddenly naked and defenseless having packed away their mechanical security blankets.

Moving down to the loading docks, they shook hands with Manuel and clambered into the dark cargo area of a truck whose refrigeration unit had been turned off. Jose threw in some old blankets to sit on and gave them several flashlights so that they could at least check the time periodically and they set off for a miserable, dark, bumpy ride to Santiago Airport. The timing proved to be just right, since as the truck slowly moved up the hill out of the city on the Santiago Highway, Jose saw that the police had pulled the limousine over and Ernesto was being questioned intently about the whereabouts of his visiting executives.

As promised, the truck lurched to a stop beside the outside entrance to a jet way where an aircraft was being serviced. A few minutes went by, then Jose quickly opened the side door of the truck, gave each descending passenger momentarily blinded by the glare of the bright sunshine a quick handshake, then hustled them up the stairs and through the jet way door which had been conveniently unlocked. Trying to brush off their suits while looking as though they belonged there, they made their way into the terminal area then slowed down and mingled with a crowd at the next gate who were excitedly greeting passengers from an arriving flight.

Moving along the concourse with the crowd, they came to the Air France gate and entered the line at the check in counter. Gar, conducting business in espanol, purchased four first class tickets to Buenos Aires with his personal credit card. The thinking was that a Rodriguez party of four on a flight to Buenos Aires would attract far less official attention during a passenger list surveillance check than a Hanley party of four booked to Los Angeles. The advantage of buying in first class, besides getting available seats, was the opportunity to wait in the first class lounge until departure. This kept them out of the public areas and allowed them to board directly from the lounge. It also provided Bill with an amazing variety of free snacks since he was in serious need of lunch. They all breathed a huge sigh of relief after they were on board, and the Air France 747 took off for the afternoon flight to Argentina.

They felt a great sense of freedom after their arrival in Buenos Aires, since for the first time in months they could assume their own identities. They cheerfully purchased travel kits, comfortable shirts and souvenirs to take home to the ladies. They also lucked out by getting four business class reservations on the 9:30 p.m. United flight to Miami, with onward connections via Chicago to Vancouver. It would take a while, but they were really on their way home. Bill hoped that Manuel would keep his promise to go to the villa, collect their suitcases, and ship them to QHRS-Vancouver since a major part of his entire wardrobe was still in Chile. They also made maximum use of the long distance telephone network to call home, using Sal's company telephone card. The arrival in Vancouver was an exciting event with plenty of people to meet them and hugs and kisses all around, despite their somewhat grubby appearance after sitting on airplanes for hours at a time.

✸
Fifty-three

I t was another rare June Saturday morning in Vancouver, sun shining and the air so clear that the North Shore Mountains seemed to be just a mile or so away. A light breeze was blowing to keep the temperature comfortable as throngs of students and their families converged at the doors of Vancouver Technical High School, eagerly anticipating the beginning of the graduation ceremony. Mr. Lewis, the principal, and his staff were hovering near the front door exchanging greetings and directing the excited students to the area where they would line up to enter the auditorium. The parents and guests also scurried along the hall and through the auditorium doors to pick out seats as close to the front as possible.

The Stuart Family arrived, Allison looking radiant, accompanied by a tall Royal Canadian Mounted Police Constable in full dress uniform. As they moved through the front entrance, Greg Calhoun, the Vancouver City Policeman assigned to school security, spotted the Mountie and noted that the red serge tunic, blue trousers, brown belt, white lanyard, and highly polished brown riding boots with spurs were immaculate. He did a double take when he recognized that Bill Patterson was the constable with Allison. He was about to rush over to congratulate Bill for joining the force just before high school graduation, then suddenly remembered that you had to earn the right to wear the dress uniform by first completing training at Depot Division. You could not possibly just sign on and then wear the uniform the next day. Greg slowly came to the realization that some sort of undercover operation had been going on right in front of his nose and he hadn't known about it. He made a mental note to talk to Bill after the ceremony and find out what had gone down. Only, of course, if Bill saw fit and was able to tell him.

After the speeches, which were accompanied by many smiles and a few tears, were over, the students came up one by one to receive their diplomas. A hush fell on the auditorium as Bill approached Mr. Lewis, came to attention and saluted. He then reached out for his diploma. Mr. Lewis held up his hands for quiet and then announced that since Bill was already a high school graduate when he arrived at Vancouver Tech., he couldn't be permitted to graduate again. Instead, he was being awarded a certificate granting him college credits for all of his course work at the school. He went on to say what a privilege it had been to have Bill as part of the student body during the day, earning top marks in academic achievement, while working so hard on other somewhat mysterious matters at night. Bill received his certificate with a grin, saluted once more, and marched to the end of the stage where he waited for Allison to receive her diploma and join him. He then escorted her back to their seats amused at the jealous glances some of the other girls were tossing at Allison.

The graduation party at the Cassidy residence was truly special. Uncle John with help from Alex Stuart continued to dish out the finest in refreshments, while Aunt Anne and Margaret Stuart circulated between the kitchen, dining room and the living room doing their utmost to ensure that everyone ate and drank more than enough. Sal had brought many good things from the warehouse for the party, in addition to the ingredients that he had previously given to John. He was enjoying the lively conversation and laughter as Margo played happily at his feet while Susan Hanley and Cheryl chatted with Allison. He had settled well into his new top management responsibilities at QHRS and the fears and concerns of the trip to Chile were gradually fading away. The daily telephone reports from the Valparaiso office were positive and the containerized produce shipments arriving three times per week were of the highest quality once again. The centerpiece on the dining room table was a tray containing a medley of the best Chilean fruit, which Sal had instructed Manuel Soto to have flown to Vancouver just yesterday.

Eventually, Bill and Allison slipped away from the crowd and out to the back porch for a few minutes of time together, cuddling, kissing and trying to absorb the meaning of what the end of one phase of their relationship and the beginning of the next might bring. This quiet time also gave Bill the chance to tell Allison that Inspector Hanley had arranged for him to be posted to the North Vancouver Detachment for field training which meant that he would be close by while Allison began at her education at Simon Fraser University. It also kept him nearby for the many meetings that would take place with the Crown Attorney during the course of several complex narcotics trial preparations. The guests began to drift away as the afternoon wore on, giving Bill and Allison the opportunity to thank the Cassidys and the Stuarts for all of their love and support during the last few months. They also made it clear that all of their future plans included a life together and earnestly solicited the support of both families in that decision.

Fifty-four

Just eighty miles southwest of the Cassidy residence where the graduation party was being enjoyed by all present, a moderate breeze blew across Esquimalt Harbor creating sun-danced ripples on the surface of the water and causing the ships secured to the pier to move gently at their moorings. It was a quiet Saturday afternoon, the Naval Ship Repair Facility shops were not open and only the occasional flash from a welder's stinger from a ship across the harbor in the dry-dock indicated that there was any activity going on in the area at all. The quarterdeck watch keepers on *HMCS Vancouver* and the other ships berthed at "A" Jetty, were somewhat surprised when a strange convoy of vehicles moved down the hill past the graving dock and moved onto the pier, pulling up beside the ship. In the lead were two RCMP patrol cruisers, followed by a fourteen-passenger van, followed by two Canadian Forces closed cargo trucks. As the Officer of the Day was called to the quarterdeck to deal with this strange phenomenon, RCMP Staff Sergeant Colin McPherson emerged from the lead cruiser followed by a work party of constables from the other cruiser and the van. The drivers of the army trucks were also RCMP personnel which was pretty unusual in itself.

Lieutenant Parker wasn't too surprised to see them all arrive, since she knew that Commander Miles was extremely anxious to get all of the special cargo off of his ship. Once again, the duty watch was piped to working stations at the quarterdeck and the sailors and constables proceeded to form a long line to progressively unload the cargo from the ship's magazine, down to the pier, and into the trucks. When the extensive cargo of mysteriously stuffed duffel bags and boxes had all been removed, signed for, and stowed away in the two trucks, five extremely subdued individuals wearing navy blue coveralls with handcuff and leg chain accessories were herded down the brow and loaded into one of the vans. When everyone and everything had been loaded and secured, the convoy drove off, leaving the ship to resume its sleepy midday weekend routine.

The RCMP convoy arrived at the BC Ferry terminal at Swartz Bay fifteen minutes before 3:00 p.m., and was waved through the toll booths, down the parking lot outside lanes past all of the waiting cars and trucks, and directly onto the lower vehicle deck of the ferry at the pier. Shortly after getting underway, ten constables escorted five coverall clad prisoners to the men's room and back, and then settled down for the rest of the trip across the Gulf of Georgia to the mainland terminal just south of Vancouver. Arriving at E-Division Headquarters just two hours later, Jorge Estaban and his traveling companions were led in to renew their acquaintanceship with Inspector Michael Hanley, who had just arrived from a delightful graduation party not far across town. The rest of the convoy then proceeded to a bonded warehouse where the cargo was unloaded from the trucks, carefully inventoried and tagged as evidence, then securely locked away.

⎈

Fifty-five

The reflection of the moon on the light chop breaking the surface of the sea indicated the direction that the cold breeze was blowing from as the waves splashed onto the Quathiaski Cove shoreline. From a car in the terminal parking lot with the front window rolled down, the sound of the diesel engines on the approaching ferry could be heard, even though the ship was still out of sight behind the point. The departure lanes in the lot had several cars lined up waiting to board the 10:00 p.m. trip to Campbell River. While too late on a Friday night for just a quick visit to Vancouver Island, obviously some folks were leaving Quadra Island for a longer weekend get away. On the other side of the lot, facing the exit lanes from the ferry ramp was a patrol car with the vehicle markings of the Royal Canadian Mounted Police. Inside the car sat Constable Level 2 Liz Hutton, who was thoroughly enjoying her recent posting to the detachment after completing an incredibly busy and hectic Field Coaching Program in Surrey Detachment. Liz, just one year and a few months away from the small town of Selkirk, Manitoba, had not liked the fast pace of the big city environment in the Vancouver Region and had usually been too tired on her days off to participate in any big city pleasures. The Quadra Island community was just the right size as far as she was concerned.

Liz was parked at the terminal to practice her skills of observation, checking for anything that seemed unusual among the people or vehicles coming off the ferry on this Friday evening in late October. While nominally there to provide assistance if required, things were still quiet on the nightwatch and it was an ideal time to advertise to any arriving visitors that there was a police presence on the island. Since tourist season was over, most visitors now came on business of one sort or another and the detachment personnel liked to stay up to date on just who was around and why. Liz was feeling just a little more important than usual tonight, since the more senior Constable Cairns and his wife were taking a long weekend off in Nanaimo leaving her as second-in-command, the only constable available to assist the NCOIC-. As the lights of the approaching ferry became visible, Liz resumed her previous thoughts about the very attractive night cook at the coffee shop by the terminal. She had developed the habit of dropping in for coffee regularly and he seemed quite friendly whenever she came in. The problem was that she was not supposed to socialize with the residents in the detachment area and she had not figured out a way to approach him with her idea of a trip to Campbell River on her day off for a dinner date.

Her daydream ended abruptly with the sound of the ferry engines going astern as the ship eased into the ramp. The lines were secured and the ramp dropped to allow the cars to slowly come ashore as she assumed her posture of casual disinterest in the unloading process. The last car to get off got her full attention. It pulled right up beside her, on the wrong side of the lane, stopping so close that she could not have opened her door to get out if she had to. As the window was rolled down, a grinning young man with a very nice looking young woman sitting beside him, asked her where all the Friday night action was in a hick town like this. Putting on her most stern patrol constable expression, Liz informed him that if he wanted some Friday night action, he had better just turn around and get his smart ass right back onto the ferry for the last trip to Campbell River.

Just as the young woman poked him and said, "Bill, don't be a tease." Liz realized who he was.

"Constable William Patterson, I have been warned about you. You had better behave yourself because your future father-in-law works as a volunteer in the detachment office on weekend evenings, answering the phone, handling radio calls and watching the cells. He was getting bored with his retirement on the island and offered to help out so that we could get more cruisers on patrol if we needed to. He mentioned that you and Allison would be coming to visit this weekend and I don't want to have to turn you over to him as being belligerent and disorderly."

"Okay, okay," laughed Bill. "Since you know who we are, why don't you let us park over there, then walk up to the café with us for a cup of coffee. Allison would like an indication of how her parents are adjusting to life on the island before we go over to see them and I could use a map or directions on how to find their place before I get hopelessly lost in this strange place."

Bill, Allison and Liz sat down at the counter and the young night cook immediately came out of the kitchen with the coffee pot in his hand and filled Liz's cup. He offered coffee to the others and then just hung around nearby as he realized that Liz knew these people and was engaged in friendly conversation. Bill finally realized what was going on and introduced himself and Allison, which then gave Liz the opportunity to introduce herself all around and learn her prospective new friend's name. Then the four of them chatted casually while Liz explained to Allison how much her parents were liked on the island. She mentioned how helpful to them that retired Sergeant Stuart was, and how many great fishing trips he and Captain Gus had together when the weather was good and the salmon were running. Liz admired Allison's engagement ring and admitted that Alex Stuart loved to tell the NCOIC of the detachment stories about his future son-in-law's adventures in undercover work, probably exaggerating about what really went on, since no one could have possibly done so much in such a short time after leaving a small farm in northern Alberta.

Bill agreed, saying he was just a young constable in training who hoped to move on to Island District to work for Inspector Hanley again some day. This conversation prompted Liz's new friend, Jim Mercer, to volunteer that he was taking a semester off from the University of Victoria to earn some money while living at home with his parents, Steve and Paula. He indicated that he intended to change his major to criminal justice and was very interested to learn about police work from Bill and, of course, Liz.

Just then, the ferry whistle blew three blasts, indicating that it was going astern to begin the trip back to Campbell River. Bill paid for the coffee, then he and Allison said "goodnight" to Jim and Liz and headed back to the car. Liz was not far behind them since she had to get back on night patrol, but she did suggest that Bill follow her to the Stuart residence since she had forgotten to draw them a map. The full moon rose higher in the night sky as peace once again settled over Quadra Island.

CPSIA information can be obtained at www.ICGtesting.com
Printed in the USA
BVOW020130290812

298966BV00001B/9/P